The Art of Drowning

by
Abigail Wild

CABLE CREEK PUBLISHING

A Cable Creek Publishing Original
Cable Creek Publishing
www.cablecreekpublishing.com

Copyright © 2020 by Abigail Wild

ISBN: (Paperback) 978-1-954064-01-0
ISBN: (Hardcover) 978-1-954064-00-3

Any references to historical events, real people, or real places are used fictitiously. Names, characters, and places are products of the author's imagination.

This book is dedicated to the memory of Scott Leith,
who was an inspiration throughout my MFA experience.
You will always be remembered.
Carry on, Space Traveler. Carry on.

When I write, my shenanigans are sometimes rather dramatic, yet somehow
my family always manages to remain supportive and inspirational.
The Art of Drowning is also dedicated to them.

Thank you, Joseph, Noah, Jacob, and Ian; together you form the light of my world.

A special note of gratitude goes out to my editor at Cable Creek: Laura, not only do you ROCK, but you found in my words the meaning I intended and found in me the strength I needed to bring this book to its completion.

I bow down in appreciation to Kelly Potteiger for the spitballs she ducked, was hit by, and threw back during my conceptual phase of planning, including the title of this novel.

I can't forget to thank JC Flynt-Wamble for taking the time to delete all my extra commas, because, I, love, commas. And, Caroline Atkins, thank you for helping Larkin survive her hospital scenes! She couldn't have done it without you.

To those who read early drafts, your courage amazes me, thank you: Trish Wild, Michaela Fetterolf, Wannette Legaspi, Nayeli Reeve, Chelle McIntyre-Brewer, and Jennifer Grybowski.

And to author Erica Wright, this book never would have happened without you. I am thankful for your help, suggestions, and patience.

Thank you!

.1.

Larkin

I needed it to stop.

Footsteps. No, stomping. Loud, earth-shattering stomping. Over and over and over again.

I started to hear talking, then yelling.

The only thing going through my mind was finding a way to escape.

I needed out.

I wasn't ready.

I wanted to go home. Back to my dark room. Back to safety.

My heart felt like it was going to force itself through my sternum. Pressure. Pain. I couldn't breathe. I felt hot. I felt like I was melting.

Drowning.

Going under.

Gasping.

I was trying to catch my breath, looking for any door I could to escape being pushed under.

My hand grabbed at the door. It was the one thing that could save me. I flailed. My hand missed its mark. That was it. I was going to drown. In public. With everyone watching, but no one seeing what was really happening.

The door flew open, throwing me forward, straight into a tall guy who was in my way. IN MY WAY. I pushed against him, jolting him sideways. I fell, knocking his papers out of his hands, scattering them in the air. I felt a sharp pain in my knee as I hit the ground. I let out a wail. The only thing I could do was cry. I sat on the ground sobbing before trying to scramble to my feet.

"What . . . just . . . Are you okay?" the tall thin monster, standing before me, asked. I had no idea who he was, but I was sure glad he wasn't Luke. "You're bleeding. Are you okay?" He spoke quickly, watching the blood drip from my knee. I fumbled to pick up his papers, dropping them over and over. I handed him a crumbled wad. I couldn't stop shaking. I could feel heat moving up through my face. Fear, embarrassment. I also couldn't help but see his cuteness. I blushed. What the actual hell? I was actually blushing. I reached down to pick up a folder, but instead I fumbled some more.

He took my hand in his. That got my attention.

"Are you okay?"

Suddenly, I could breathe. I was saved from drowning; air filled my lungs. Gasping, I looked into his eyes and something completely different took over. I had made a fool of myself in front of this stranger.

"Yeah, um, yes," I said. I looked down at my bleeding knee. What a great way to start my senior year. It was fan-freaking-tastic. I quickly grabbed the rest of the papers, handed them to him, and started to plan my escape. "Thank you," I muttered. I could feel him staring at me. I lifted my eyes to take a quick peek. He looked shocked and concerned.

Behind this stranger, I could see Luke walk past the door. Luke who had forgotten me so quickly as if we'd never been together at all. Luke! Three years meant nothing to him. My stomach dropped.

"Larkin, there you are," a voice from behind me said. Startled, I turned.

Dr. Smith was standing there with a smile. She put her hand on my back to try to steady me. "Let's go chat in my office. I would love to catch up with you, and maybe help you clean up your knee." She turned around to look at the tall guy. "Thanks Marco, I'll take her from here." Now I was an object to be traded. Great, that didn't make me feel like a loser AT ALL.

***

Drowning? There's an art to it, you know. Sometimes the world falls apart and you are left gasping for air. Other times it's a peaceful thing, like you want to stay there and let the water fill your lungs. Whether peaceful or terrifying, it always leaves you gasping at the end. Death never comes for me, but the drowning is always present.

That morning it had seemed so surreal being out of the house. The sun was just peeking out over the tree line ahead. Little kids were at their bus stops with their moms standing behind, drinking their morning coffee and gossiping about who knows what. For them it was the first day of school. For me though? It was entirely different. It was my first day back at school in two years.

I thought back to my first day of Kindergarten. Erin and I had run from our front doors and raced all the way to the end of the street, laughing the entire time. We were so excited to start school that we'd been playing at it for a whole year to get ready. Erin had worn a white sequined shirt, pink skirt with a layer of tulle overtop, and, as always, a tiara. She wanted everyone, everywhere to know she would be a famous ballerina someday. Me? I'd had on a green shirt, sky blue pants, and white pleather kitten heals.

I was so sad when Erin moved away in fourth grade. I mourned what we had when we were small. It was perfect. It was pure. Not like that day, when a school bell sent me into a panic throwing me to the ground amidst a pack of high school seniors. I'd grown up to become the All-State Soccer goalie in my freshman year. I was even being scouted for Penn State. IN FRESHMAN YEAR. But much like everyone else, Penn State stopped contacting me after the accident during the summer before sophomore year. All it took to destroy my dream was getting kicked in the head at a soccer tournament. They said my concussion would heal. *"You should be better in about a week."* Yeah right. *"It'll be no time until you get back on the field!"* These things were always said with fake smiles. When they realized I wasn't healing, they started going on and on about how Post-Concussion Syndrome wasn't that bad. *Shows what they knew.* The injury reset my life. I wasn't the same Larkin. There was no way I could be. Two years spent in a dark bedroom recovering had brought me to this moment. My senior year.

.2.

Reagan

The bell blasted. I reached out from under my covers to silence it. My alarm clock blaring was not how I pictured starting my senior year. Why hadn't I woken up early, before the alarm? Soccer practice, that's why. The night before had been brutal. My legs felt like cement. My arms cramped. Something had crawled up Coach Toan's butt the night before. He was mad at us for losing our first game, so he went hard on us. I swear we must have been planking for an hour. Coach was being an ass. We lost one game—our first game of the season—so what?! I hadn't wanted us to lose either, but that was no excuse for working us like that.

I climbed out of bed and started my routine to get ready for school. It was the first day of my senior year, but I wasn't worried about it; I had it all together.

My SATs were done. I had already committed to play soccer for Stone Valley University and all of my hard classes were out of the way. I was done! While everyone else crammed for their SATs and college apps, all I had to do was sit back and relax with my boyfriend, Luke. I wiped the condensation from the mirror as I continued going through the list in my head. I sighed in relief, then flashed a smile at my reflection.

I was done! The rest was easy. Everything was wrapped up for me.

My mom had been on my ass all these years, but I hit every mark she set for me.

I hoped maybe she would be proud of me.

I pulled on my clothes, a ripped pair of jeans, dark blue t-shirt, and light blue Converse. I didn't want to look like I cared too much. I threw my straight hair up into a ponytail, spread some gloss over my lips and voila! I smiled at myself before turning downstairs to get some breakfast.

"What the hell are you wearing?" My mom's voice sounded like booming thunder. Her voice was always jarring; never caring. She stood before me with her perfectly straight brown bobbed hair, Kate Spade tortoise shell glasses, and her perfectly altered Armani suit with a Hermes scarf around her neck.

"Mom, I just want to be comfortable," I said back. I just wanted her to lay off.

"Reagan, go change your clothes. Comfort does not equal success. And another thing," my mom said with her hand on her hip, "do you think you'll be able to keep Luke this way? Hell no."

"MOM!"

"I see the way he looks at other girls; look better than them. Get changed. And for God sake, would it hurt you to wear a little lip gloss?" she snapped.

"Fine." I turned and stomped to my bedroom, then slammed the door shut.

"Do not slam your door at me, young lady!" she yelled.

"Fine!" I yelled through the door.

I threw on a pair of khaki capris and a silky black shirt that I thought might make her happier. I looked at myself one more time and decided to add a necklace just to be sure I was presentable enough. My hands shook as I worked its clasp.

I tried to go down to get breakfast, but instead my mother met me at the top of the steps. "Here, I made you a green shake."

"Thanks?" I took the silver thermos she thrust in front of me. "I think I'll make myself a waffle too."

"Reagan, you've gained weight this summer. You need to stop eating. Drink it."

"Mom! I didn't gain. I made sure to use the running schedule you made me." I never met my father, but he must not be as thin as my mom. I'd never be as skinny as her. It had to be genetics.

I took a sip of the green shake and almost choked. God, it tasted awful.

"Look at yourself; your pants are snug. Trust me, you'll thank me."

"Whatever."

"Are you sure you don't want to actually do something to your hair?"

"Mom, no. I'm fine," I protested. "Luke will be here soon."

Without saying goodbye, my mother turned around, grabbed her Birkin bag, looked at me with a sigh of disgust, and left the house.

"Bye, mom. Love you too," I said to no one. "Awe thanks, Mom! You have a good day too!" I rolled my eyes, took another sip of the shake, and grabbed my bag.

As I walked out of my house, Luke pulled into the driveway. He didn't get out to kiss me or anything. He usually wasn't so caring if people weren't watching. Whatever, it was fine, it didn't bother me. *I lied to myself, of course it bothered me.* I jumped into the passenger side.

"Hey babe," Luke said. He leaned over to give me a quick kiss on my cheek. "What's that?" he asked, pointing to my thermos. "Because I know your mom isn't letting you have coffee."

"Green shake," I said with a sneer. "I guess I'm too fat for a waffle now."

"Well, I'm into your fat… so." He flashed me a smirk.

"Butthead," I said, playfully punching him in the arm. He acted as if I hurt him terribly, pulling away from me and rubbing his shoulder.

"Next year we'll be away from this crap, and you can eat as many waffles as you want." He winked at me.

"Nope, freshman fifteen," I said in a sing-song voice.

I was so excited about us going to college together. Our relationship might not have been perfect, but the fact that I had him really made me feel good about myself. Together we were a powerful force. Everyone talked about us, everyone loved us, everyone wished they were us. I saw the way the freshman looked at him, but he was mine. In my mind, there was no reason that wouldn't carry over to college.

We didn't talk the rest of the way to school. We didn't need to. We were like an old couple, the type of couple that was comfortable enough to sit quietly. No pressure. At least that's what I told myself.

As we pulled into the school, I could spot all the different groups of upperclassmen hanging out at their cars while the busses held the under-classmen hostage. I still remember the athletes near the tennis courts and the nerds by the big oak tree. The goths stood beside the building. The theater kids sat on Leo's car. Leo was always our lead male and was always dramatic. Plus, he was better at make-up than I was; stage makeup was seri-ous business. If I needed to gossip, it was him I found. If dirty work needed to be done, I could count on him. He was my low-key wing man.

The morning bell hadn't rung yet, so Luke and I had time to hang out. Luke pulled into his newly assigned spot and we began to put on our show. We kissed, a long drawn out kiss. Just for show. I looked around to see if anyone noticed. They noticed; they all did. Having a hot guy like Luke hold me closely only added to the power I held over everyone.

We got out of Luke's Jeep and went our separate ways.

"Izzy! Hey girl!" I said to our team's tall red headed midfielder. "How are you feeling after last night's workout?"

"O . . . M . . . G . . . I can barely walk," Izzy said. She rubbed her thighs. "I swear Coach hates us!"

"Right?" I laughed, taking a sip of my shake.

"You have some green stuff on your lip." She pointed to the center of her top lip.

"Oh yeah," I said with a nod. "I've decided to pay more attention to my health." I wiped my mom's green disaster off my face. "You know self-care and all that."

"Good for you. I should start doing that. Give me your recipe!"

"What recipe?" Brooke asked as she walked up to us. Brooke and I had a stressed relationship. It didn't help that she was Larkin's best friend.

"Reagan's doing a juice cleanse," Izzy answered.

"Cool!" Brooke looked at me dismissively. "So, who is coming to my pool party?

"Luke and I wouldn't dream of missing it." I tried to sound excited.

"Wonderful," Brooke said with the hint of a sigh.

"Izzy, come with me to buy a new bikini before the party?" I asked.

Izzy pushed her hair off her shoulder, "Who am I to say no to shopping?"

Brooke looked at us, rolled her eyes, and walked away to tell others about the party. She was inviting the entire senior class.

The bell rang, letting us know we needed to get our butts inside. Luke snuck up behind me and grabbed my shoulders trying to scare me. He didn't scare me; I could see his shadow, but I certainly jumped as if he did. We walked into the building hand in hand, as expected, and made our way through the hallway lined with maroon lockers. Teachers stood around making sure traffic flowed.

A group of freshman girls stared at Luke. I tried not to look at them, but they lined my peripheral vision. I made sure to give Luke a small peck on his cheek as we passed by. *He's mine, stay away! Don't forget that!* I smiled at them coyly.

"Okay, we have second and fifth period together," I said. "Meet me at my locker before then. Oh, and before lunch! Don't forget!"

"Of course!" Luke replied.

I looked at Luke and smiled. When he smiled back, I tried to find a caring spark in his eyes. With perfect timing he squeezed my hand, which showed me he really did love me. I might have loved him more than he loved me, but there was something there. I smiled, then bit my lower lip a little just because it always drove him insane.

Suddenly, someone caught my attention in the guidance office. I turned to see a girl crying while Dr. Smith tried to help her. Strange! Outbursts like that didn't usually happen at the beginning of the year.

I looked more closely: long curly hair, dressed in black, mascara running down her face. That's when I realized! It was Larkin. A litany of swear words sprang to mind, I struggled to keep them from escaping my lips. She looked awful. She was terribly skinny, pale, and she seemed scared. I had to tell myself not to stare. Not to make any more of a scene than she was already making. I needed to look away, but I also needed to know what was going on. Why was she back? *Shit!* I thought she was gone forever. It was at that moment that I felt it all start to slip from my fingers.

I grabbed Luke's hand tighter and tried to lead him away before he noticed her.

"What's wrong, ba . . ." He stopped walking and stared through the guidance office window. He looked as if he was staring at a ghost. Hell, he turned so white that he actually looked like he was a ghost. I still had a hold of his hand as I pulled him along behind me. "Was that? Is that?" Luke began to ask.

"It's Larkin, yes. Come on, don't worry about her," I said. It was impossible to get him moving again. I could not believe this was happening.

Please, dear God, don't let her be back.

She was probably just picking up paperwork. There's no way she was staying. Who would come back just for their last year? But, even if she did stay, she was no threat. She was so skinny. She looked sick. But, damn it, I wished Luke wasn't staring at her. I wanted to scream, STOP STARING AT HER, but I didn't. And he didn't stop staring.

I finally got him away from the office window so he couldn't see her anymore. I tried to look into his eyes, but they looked lost. He was not there; he was trapped in a memory with her.

"Babe!" I tried to get his attention; I even snapped my fingers in front of his face. He gave no sign that he heard me or that he cared to hear me. I took his face in my hands and looked directly into his eyes, but he looked away. "Babe, it's okay. You have me now." I pleaded with him to notice me. "You don't need her, you have me. Just look at me!" I was still pleading but he didn't even react. My heartrate spiked and I felt my cheeks get hot. "Luke, I'm standing here right in front of you, COME ON!" Nothing. He just turned and walked away.

I started to hear her name in the hallway; everyone was excited to see her. I noticed Brooke walking down the hall with a huge smile on her face; her usually spirited walk even more energetic. She didn't know Larkin was coming back? She didn't say anything. I couldn't believe this was happening. It felt like a bad dream. I slammed my locker shut.

. 3 .

Larkin

I found my way to the girls' restroom and stared in horror at my reflection. I looked like the height of 90's grunge. I was a complete mess. Once I got myself looking somewhat human again, I pulled out my schedule. AP Lit and Creative Writing. Thank God for small favors.

The bell shrieked again. It was loud, but this time I was prepared. I didn't think I was ready for the crowded halls, so I decided to wait. Luckily, no one entered the restroom. My breathing was heavy and long, but overall, I felt okay.

"It's time," I whispered to myself. I grabbed my bag. The halls were crowded with the excitement of the first day. Lockers slammed, new kids wandered lost, groups of friends chattered in clusters along the walls. Two guys tossed a nerf ball back and forth "going long" over the heads of the kids in the hall.

But I walked alone, slightly hunched over, arms crossed tightly in front of me. I looked at the ground, making myself as small as possible and hoping no one would notice me. Then I heard it.

"Larkin! Hey Larkin!" Reagan walked up to me. "I had no idea you'd be back!" She was always jealous of me and wanted my spot on the varsity team. She constantly did things to try to make me look bad. It never worked. But that was before, I was not that same Larkin anymore.

"Hey, Reagan! It's . . . good to see you," I lied.

"So, what made you come back THIS year?"

"The doctor cleared me."

"Cleared you? For everything? Even soccer?" she asked, but before I could answer she leaned in close and whispered in my ear, "Please don't think you'll be getting your position back, I've done great things; you failed us."

It's amazing how some people can smile while sounding so hateful. Unsettling.

"Besides, look at you. You're tiny now. I thought you'd be working out more on your . . . break." She looked me up and down with a fake smile on her face.

My stomach dropped. I reminded myself to breathe. I couldn't believe she was being so bold. So quickly. Let's be honest, she only became goalie because of my injury; she needed to remember that, but I was in no position to remind her. All I wanted to do was get through the day.

"Anyway, I'm so happy to see you!" she leaned in and gave me a fake hug. "Welcome back!" She squealed.

"Larky!!!!!" Brooke jumped in front of us with her practice jersey on. "OMG, Lark, is that really you?"

"Brooke!!!!" I said with a sigh of relief. She was my best friend before the injury. She was always such a happy person. I couldn't help but think, *why couldn't you have visited me? Why did you leave me alone?* But we hugged each other tightly. Hugging her felt like a sanctuary from the onslaught of Reagan.

Reagan squealed again. "I know! I'm so excited she's back! Can you just believe it?"

Brooke ignored Reagan. "Hey, Coach Toan asked me to help him coach his eight-year old girls' team. I think he's looking for another student coach. We should do it together!"

"Um, maybe?" I said, "He's probably forgotten me, anyway."

"Nah, he always talks about how you were the best goalie he ever had," Brooke said. "It will be fun! I'll talk to him."

"Whatever." Reagan said. She turned on her heal and stomped away, obviously angry.

"Where are you going now?" asked Brooke.

"AP Calc."

"Okay? That sounds like hell! Let's eat lunch together today, okay? We have so much to talk about." Typical Brooke, she waved her hands around while she talked. "I'm so happy you're back," she shrieked, as if she hadn't forgotten my existence for two years.

"Okay, save me a spot," I said. It seemed like old times and even looked like old times, but I couldn't trust it, you don't get over feeling abandoned with just a smile.

I found my classroom and slowly went in. The room was blinding. Bright lights. Eggshell walls. It felt like an assault. The smell of the whiteboard markers overwhelmed me. It all made my headache just a little bit worse. Still, at least I was out of the hallway. Equations from the last period were still scrawled on the board. Even as everyone walked into the room, it was quieter than being in the hallway. I felt like the pressure was off of me, despite the bright lights. I had a sweet 55 minutes of not having to worry about loud sounds and people recognizing me. Even if that time was filled with functions and equations, it would still be better than the chaos of the halls.

I knew exactly what was being taught and began raising my hand to answer questions. In fact, math-wise I was on top of the world. I had always felt so behind in math, but not then. It was amazing . . . and strange. I didn't know if it was because I had had a personal tutor for the past two years or if this was another positive effect of the head injury. You know, like that guy who was in a bar fight and woke up speaking perfect Mandarin? What were the chances? When you heal from a head injury, some things can go in a strange direction. Sometimes it's your personality, sometimes it's your intellect, and sometimes it's your beliefs. You never come back the same as before. That was certainly true for me.

I took a quick look around the room. I remembered some of the peo-ple, but I had never hung out with any of them. They were mostly people I made fun of. I felt like I was being thrust into another world, one that I had never seen myself being a part of.

I continued to look around, and there he was. Marco. He wasn't here during Freshman year. Where did he come from? He gave me a quick glance, then a smirk. Of course, he smirked; I had made an ass out of my-self in front of him that morning. A lot of emotions and thoughts hit me all at once. There was something about him, but I couldn't figure out what it was. I wanted to sit and stare at him, but I had to look away. Was it because he was kind to me when I was freaking out? Or was it because I just wanted him?

Oh my God, his beautifully unkempt, dark hair, and the way he ran his fingers through it when thinking, was just . . . hot. He looked up and noticed that I was still looking at him. I was being completely creepy, and he knew it. But he didn't seem bothered. I think he even blushed a little bit. He flashed me the biggest smile, then looked down at his paper again. I turned around quickly, holding my breath. I was a teenage cliché.

Time was up. I held my hands over my ears. Even though I could still hear the bell, holding my ears grounded me. Everyone else grabbed their bags and headed to their next class. I decided to take my time to avoid the crowd. I put my book and notebook into my bag slowly so I could waste time.

"Um. Hi. I've been worried about what happened earlier. I can't get it out of my head." His dark brown eyes looked at me intently. His eyebrows furrowed with worry. Then he gave me the same kind, endearing smile he had when he caught me looking at him. I could feel myself go flush. I zipped my bag and he bent over and picked it up for me.

"Oh . . . th-thank you." I knew I was bright red; I could feel my cheeks burning. "I'm okay. It's just my first day back in two years," I said as I dropped my pencil. "I was, sort of, nervous, I guess." I stood up. He handed me my bag. My fingers brushed against his and that's when I felt something I hadn't felt in a long time. Attraction.

"Two years off? I would love to hear more about that, but right now, we have to get to class." He put his hand out, "My name is Marco. It's nice to meet you."

"Larkin," I said as he shook my hand. I noticed his hands were calloused and his eyes were incredibly intense. At first glance, there was nothing remarkable about him, but being close enough to shake his hand showed there was more there than you could ever imagine. I felt hot again; I knew I was blushing.

"Larkin? Interesting name. It sounds familiar." He looked in the air and placed his pointer finger on his chin. "Ah yes, wasn't there a poet who wrote about your parents messing you up?"

My eyes widened; he was talking about Philip Larkin. I had never come upon anyone who knew Philip Larkin, at least not outside of my own family. "Yeah, Philip Larkin. *This be the Verse* is one of my favorites." I raised my eyebrows. "How do you know about him? He's not someone we read in school."

"I love reading. What a strange man to be named after, Larkin."

"What's the one about deprivation?" I asked. I was testing him now.

"Right, where he talks about Wordsworth," he replied.

"Wow." I took a step back with wide eyes, "I'm . . . shocked!" I could feel my smile growing. "I've never met anyone who every knew about Philip Larkin. Not even any teachers have mentioned my name."

"I would love to meet your parents and ask them what they were thinking, naming their daughter after an eccentric poet like Larkin." He stood back and crossed his arms in front of him. He looked at me for a moment with small grin before he turned and left the room.

I couldn't help but smile. I wanted to know who he was. I needed to know everything about him. He was different from everyone else, in jeans and t-shirt, which seemed normal enough, but the backwards flat cap he wore set him apart. You know that kind old men wear? He had these intense eyes. Like, when he looked at you, he could see into your soul. His eyes gave me the shivers.

I finally left the room with little time to spare. That's when it happened, I ran into Luke, my ex-boyfriend. We never technically broke up; he just ghosted me after my injury. He didn't want to hang out with an invalid, apparently. Who would? Not Luke, that's for sure.

He was wearing a polo golf shirt, jeans, and black Adidas Samba Classics. His brown was hair was spiked in the front with so much product that it looked wet. I had forgotten how cute he actually was. What I had not forgotten was how vain he had always been. He knew he was hot.

"Larkin!" He looked surprised. I needed to remind myself to breathe.

"Hey Luke." I gave him a very small smile; if you happened to blink, you would have missed it.

"I didn't know you were coming back to school . . . ever." He looked a little nervous, but I have to admit, that 'ever' really stung.

"Well, here I am," I said as I reminded myself to breathe.

"Great! We'll have to do some catching up." He actually winked at me.

"Luke, there you are!" It was Reagan. She threaded her arm through his and stretched up to give him a kiss on the cheek. *WOW! Alrighty then.* This was one more piece of evidence to show how completely out of the loop I really was.

"Oh, Hi Larkin," she said. "Luke, did you notice Larkin was back?" It felt like she was talking about me as if I were a two-year-old! By then, I was far too pissed to even have a panic attack, but I kept smiling.

"Wow, Reagan, I think it's so wonderful that you basically took over my life! Good for you; you always wanted it so badly." To this day, I still can't believe that I said that OUT LOUD with that huge smile plastered all over my face.

"Whatever, Larkin," she said, rolling her eyes.

. 4 .

Reagan

I couldn't believe it was happening. I worked so hard to get where I was, and she just waltzed in to take it all back. I took a deep breath and let it out slowly. Looking in the girls' room mirror, I began to realize my mom was right. I should have done a better job on my hair. I should have done more for my makeup. I should have run every day. I shouldn't have had those chips this weekend. I shouldn't have been born with these weak genetics. I was never enough; my mom was right. She was always right.

"Compose yourself," I said to my reflection, and took another deep breath. I knew if I flipped out, I would push Luke away.

I took my hair out of its bun. I pushed my fingers through it as it fell around my face. Then I flipped my head upside down and ran my fingers through it again, desperately trying to give it more body. When I came back up, I looked in the mirror again.

"Not enough!" I snapped at my reflection. I grabbed my backpack and rummaged through the front pocket pulling out a tube of mascara and lip gloss. I carefully swiped more mascara on my lashes, trying to make them longer, and applied a nude colored gloss to my lips. I put the tubes away and looked in the mirror again.

"Better, but not perfect," I whispered to myself. There was no way I would keep his attention. Even after two years he still missed her. I could see it in his eyes.

Suddenly the girls' room door flew open. A group of three came in like a tornado of activity, laughing and gossiping. I quickly grabbed my bag to get out of there. The last thing I needed was for them to notice that I was upset.

"Did you see Larkin yet?" the girl in the black hoodie asked.

I couldn't get away from hearing about her. I couldn't figure out what made her so special. Why did they have to be talking about her?

"O-M-G! I did. I'm so happy she's back!" a girl in a swim team hoodie said.

"I know, right?"

I threw my backpack on and whipped past, practically knocking into them. "Watch it! What's your problem?" the girl in the hoodie snapped.

I didn't turn around to say anything; I just kept going. My stomach was knots.

I took a deep breath, brushed my hair off my shoulder, lifted my head and started walking, ignoring my own evil thoughts.

I found Luke the moment I turned out of the restroom. He was putting books into his locker. I ran up, practically bouncing on top of him. Anything to get his attention.

"Hey baby!" I said, but he didn't look at me, so I started running my fingers under his hairline on his neck, something that always got his attention. Still nothing. I needed to do more.

Finally, he took a deep breath.

"Sorry, I'm just not here right now. Let's meet up at lunch, okay?" He quickly kissed my cheek and walked away.

What the hell? We were going to the same class and he just walked away from me. "Izzy! What's up, girl?" I yelled out to the tall blonde in front of me.

She turned, "Hey! So, I'm thinking about a Target run for the bikinis. Want to come with me on Saturday? Before the party?"

"Yeah! Perfect!" I responded while trying to get my thoughts off of Luke. I was just happy she didn't bring up Larkin.

"Are you worried?" Izzy asked.

"Worried about finding the right bikini at the end of the season? Yep!" I replied, but my stomach sank. I knew what she meant. I wasn't stupid.

"No, are you worried Larkin will go after Luke?"

"Oh, her? Did you see her? She looks like a skeleton," I said. My heart rate quickened. "He knows what I do for him."

"Yeah, he would be crazy!"

"Exactly."

We entered the classroom, where I saw Luke was already sitting deep in thought with his leg bouncing under the desk. I sat next to him like I always did.

"Hey, babes, you okay?"

He looked at me with those shining blue eyes that always pierced right through me, "Yeah."

I decided to just lay it on the line with him, "I know it's hard seeing her again."

He took a deep breath. "Mmm hmm."

"Have you talked to her again?"

"No."

I sighed deeply.

Mrs. Turner walked in, her high heels clicking with every step.

"Welcome back, everyone. Let's get right to it. Pass your summer homework to the front of the room."

I pulled the packet of papers out of my folder and handed them ahead, but I couldn't actually concentrate on class. I was too anxious. It was only a matter of time before they talked again.

Finally, after an hour stewing in my thoughts, not paying attention at all, the bell rang. I grabbed my bag, but by the time I threw it on my back, Luke was gone.

. 5 .

Larkin

It was time for lunch, but the thought of the lunchroom terrified me. I was sure I wasn't ready for that much noise, or that many people all in one place. I wasn't even hungry. What was the point? And I didn't want to run into Reagan and Luke. I kept telling myself I wasn't bothered, but that was a lie. I knew my limits and being in that cafeteria was well past them.

"Larkin! How are you, dear?"

"Well, I'm here! So, that's good," I replied to the older, chubby woman in pink scrubs who stood in front of me. "My mom asked me to come and see you. She wants to make sure you're up to date in case anything happens."

"Oh yes, I had a lovely conversation with your mother just this morning." *Because of course she did.* "Is this your lunchtime?"

"Yeah, but I'm not hungry."

"Mmm-Hmm, I'll just call down to the lunchroom and have someone bring you some lunch." I didn't want to think about food. When I heard her say that she talked to my mom, I should have known she'd try to make me eat.

"No, that's okay. I'm fine."

"Really, it's no bother. You look a little pale, and skinny. Let me feed you." Yep, she definitely talked to my mother. "We'll just sit and chat while you eat. They can bring me something as well; I need the break. It will be lovely." She picked up the phone to make a call.

"Yes, hello. Could you please send two lunches to the nurses office?" she asked, smiling at me. "Of course, the special is fine. Thank you." She hung up and gestured for me to sit at the table. "Come sit down, tell me how everything is going so far."

"I think it's going well. I'm not sure there's really anything to talk about."

"Okay, well, let's start with why you didn't want to go to the lunch-room?"

"My mom just wanted me to come and talk to you today. I thought this was the best time." I tried to plead my case.

"Most of the students want to go to lunch, but you chose to spend that time with me. What's going on?"

"Well, to be honest, I'm not good with a ton of sound or large groups of people. They give me," I paused, "panic attacks." I answered. She nodded at me in a knowing way.

"I understand. It will take some time." She nodded again. "You had a traumatic event, followed by what can only be described as solitary confine-ment." She hit the nail on the head with that statement.

"It was hard, but I'm back," I paused. "I'm back and I'm going to make the best of it." The door swung open. A hair-netted cafeteria lady in a white apron entered carrying two lunches. The smell that wafted around her could only be described as vomit inducing drek.

"Oh goody, Larkin, it's mystery meat day, yummmm," Nurse Susan said, rolling her eyes. The cafeteria lady grimaced, making me hold in a laugh. "Well, the only thing we can do now is dig in." We both held up our mini milks to toast. "To a good school year, full of good memories, good food, and no panic attacks."

"Cheers." I answered back.

I immediately fell into the habit of pushing food around my plate to make it look as if I was eating. I took tiny bites and chewed them forever. I drank from my water bottle as much as humanly possible. I started look-ing around for a trash can, hoping I could throw some of it away without her noticing, but there wasn't one close enough. So, I started my next trick. Talking. A lot. If I talked a lot, no one really noticed that I wasn't eating.

"Larkin, you know that to become better, you are going to have to eat. You went through a lot and you still have some healing to do, food fuels that," she chastised me. I stared at my plate. "Not only that, but your panic attacks might get better if you have some food in you." I looked up at her. "I know this could be a control thing for you. You've felt helpless for so long. I understand that."

"That's what my doctors said."

"Larkin, you don't want to end up in the hospital."

Why did my mother have to tell everyone everything? I had to make a decision. Throw away the food and walk out? Or stay and eat that one meal, then skip dinner. I began eating tiny bites in the hopes she would become occupied with something else. So, I willed myself to keep talking, about anything.

"Any exciting programs this year?" I asked, but I didn't listen to her answer. I was too busy calculating the caloric intake of every bite. I was determined to stay below 500 calories for the day.

I knew the meatloaf would sit like a brick in my stomach all afternoon and I couldn't fathom the number of calories that were in that little brown lump of disgustingness. I couldn't have all this food inside of me, but she wasn't about to let me go without eating something. That's when I thought about purging for the first time, but I quickly got it out of my mind. Making myself throw up was too gross. Puking my guts out on purpose was a line I wasn't willing to cross. Yet. I got through about a quarter of my food, but then I just couldn't eat anymore. I took a deep breath and a drink of my water bottle. If I took one more bite, I'd throw up without meaning to. I felt nauseated. Luckily, the phone rang, and she had to turn her back to answer it. That's when I took half of what was left on my tray and scooped it into a baggie I had put in my backpack that morning. When she turned around, I acted like I was chewing while I packed up my things and gathered my bag for the next class. It worked out perfectly.

"Thank you, Larkin. You've made my day today. I'm proud of you," she said, noting my empty plate. Imagine being congratulated for eating, I felt like a child. I gave her a small smile. "The bell is going to ring soon. Are you okay to go on with your day? How's your headache?"

"It's about a 3 on the 1 to 10 scale, which is pretty good for me. I'll come down if it gets to a five."

"Perfect. Can I count on you for lunch tomorrow?" she asked.

"I'll let you know," I answered, knowing full well that if I went back for lunch, she would make me eat. Bag in hand, I cleaned up my plate and turned to leave a little early so I would have a moment to collect myself before the bell rang.

"Oh, Larkin?" she said with a sweet smile. I turned to look at her. "I just want you to know that I think you are beautiful. The mirror lies."

.6.

Reagan

The lunchroom was loud. I kept hearing Larkin's name, but she wasn't there. While in line, Luke kept turning and looking around for her, I could tell he was agitated, with his darting eyes. I couldn't take any more of his display, so I took his face in my hands and turned his head in my direction.

"Luke, look at me. We are happy. We are in charge of this place. I'm here. I've been here. Don't pull away from me," I pleaded. My hands fell to his waist.

"I'm not. What are you talking about?" He rolled his eyes then quickly shot a look around the room looking for her. "You're acting crazy." His eyes darted back and forth searching.

"No, you are thinking about her. I can tell."

"I am not!" He practically shouted. "I'm thinking about the game tonight. That's all. Get over yourself!" I could see his chest breathing in and out, but when he looked at me, his eyes softened. The red in his face went away as he said, "Baby, I'm sorry. You're right. Seeing her just threw me off."

"Just keep looking to me. Okay?" I said. "We've grown so much together. We've shared so much." I put my hands to his chin and held him there, eyes locked with mine.

"What the hell are you doing?"

My stomach fell. "What do you mean?"

He pushed my hands away and said, "What is all this? Touching my face as if I just got some deadly disease."

I knew at that moment she was the disease, a fatal virus for our relationship. "Babe, I just. I don't know." I took a step back. "You aren't yourself."

"You're just being crazy."

"No."

"Stop being crazy," he snapped at me, then turned and walked away. He found some of his teammates to sit with; leaving me standing there, feeling completely alone in a sea of people.

"What the hell was that?" said Izzy, who was suddenly next to me.

"Larkin."

"I saw she was back."

"Right, well. That's what's wrong with him." I walked away not saying anything more. I didn't want to talk to anyone.

.7.

Larkin

The halls were quiet again. I could breathe easily. I loved those brief solitary moments, no matter how fleeting they were. Then I heard it.

"Larkin! You weren't at lunch." I turned to see Brooke coming from a few feet away.

"Hey, Brooke, sorry. I had an appointment."

"Well, that sounds serious! What are you up to tonight? Some of us are going to Al's for Pizza. I think you should come."

"I don't know. I have to get extra sleep. I don't want my headaches to return."

"Oh, yeah." She looked dumbfounded. "So, why didn't you come back sooner? I've missed you."

I couldn't believe she said that. The whole time I was sick, she never even texted me. I would have LOVED for her to pop by, but she didn't. How could she say she missed me when she could have called me at any time?

"The injury was a lot worse than they thought, it took a while for me to heal," I said, shrugging. I didn't know what else to say.

"Oh, well, I hope you can make it tonight," she said, then turned and walked away.

I noticed the time and held my hands over my ears, bracing myself. The bell rang and everyone flooded the halls. Even with my ears plugged, I expected the bell to send my headache off the charts, but it didn't; I actually felt okay. I felt like I had a brick in my stomach after lunch, but I was really okay. I was conquering something evil and finally winning. I breathed in triumph and steeled myself for whatever came next.

I walked the hallway, weaving in and out of the commotion, on my way to Creative Writing. That was the class I expected to become my favorite. The only problem was that the teacher was my dad's friend, Mr. Parson, or "Paul" around my house. That meant that he knew ALL about me. Of course, I'm pretty sure my mother had already spoken to all my teachers anyway, but when I was recovering, Mr. Parson had a front seat view of all that happened. At least I knew that he was in my corner, but, really, I just wanted to move past it all. I wanted to be normal again. The last thing I needed from him was conversation and understanding. This was school. I just wanted him to be my teacher, my regular teacher. It felt weird.

When I got to class, Mr. Parson was sitting at his desk. He was always so handsome; I couldn't imagine my dad hanging out with him in high school. With our families spending so much time together, I didn't feel like I could get personal in my writing. I couldn't trust that he wouldn't go to my parents with every little poem that I wrote. Naturally, I ended up being right. That's exactly what he did.

His face lit up when he saw me. "Larkin! I'm excited to have you in my classes this year!" he said. This man watched me grow up. This man babysat me. It was weird.

"Hey, Mr. Parson!"

I turned to find a seat and saw Marco furiously writing something in a sketchbook. My heart skipped a beat. He looked up and smiled at me, then looked back down at his writing. I wondered what he was doing. Whatever it was, it seemed extremely important. Passion like that is intoxicating. He was intoxicating.

"Larkin, over here!" A familiar voice called to me from the opposite side of the room, "Larkin!"

I turned around slowly. It was Luke. I was really trying to re-acclimate myself to this new, this old life. But you know what? He forgot me, so forget him. I looked at him and smiled. "I'm sorry Luke, I actually need to talk to Marco about, a-, a project."

Luke narrowed his eyes and whispered under his breath, "That freak?" He looked down at his desk. I rejected the impulse to say anything and simply turned around.

"You chose to sit next to me, instead of the handsome Luke McAvoy? Interesting."

"Yeah, well, I've had enough of pompous egos for a while," I replied.

Marco smirked at me and continued his writing. Not looking up from his sketchbook, he said, "I feel very humbled. And you don't even know me that well. For all you know, I have a pompous ego too."

"Yes, I'm sure, the pompiest of pomposity."

"Indeed." He let out a small laugh.

"Larkin, could you please come up here?" Mr. Parson called. I knew how this was going to go. *How are you feeling?*

"How are you feeling?"

"I'm doing well, no major headache or anything."

Did you eat lunch?

"Did you get some lunch?"

I had this conversation so many times before, I knew exactly what he was going to say. Everyone always said it, all the time.

"Yes, I ate with the nurse."

If you need anything . . .

"Okay, great. If you need anything, my door is always open. I'm here for you, Larkin, I really am." He put his arm gently on my shoulder.

"Thank you, Mr. Parson," I said, then turned and walked back to my seat.

Marco gave me a side eye. "Friends with the teacher?" He teased.

I felt a tap on my shoulder. Luke towered over me. "Larkin, you should come and sit with me, not this loser," he said.

Um.

"Thanks Luke, but like I said, I am working on something with Marco."

Reagan walked in the door to the classroom. When she saw Luke standing over me, her eyes grew wide, her mouth closed, and her lips went thin.

"Luke," she said in a huff. Luke turned around and began to walk away. Before he got very far, he turned back one last time, pointed at Marco, and said, "I'm just saying, he's a freak."

Marco didn't seem to care, or even notice the way Luke was behaving towards him. If someone stood there and said that about me? It would have definitely started a panic attack.

I could see Reagan in my peripheral vision. She gave me a few dirty looks, but she mostly sat and watched Luke. The more Luke looked at me, the more Reagan got mad. Her face turned red and her leg bounced up and down like crazy. I couldn't believe how everyone was acting. I was INJURED, hello! They were so wrapped up in their own minds and drama, they couldn't even see that.

Luke was confused, that much was clear. It was obvious he couldn't understand why I was not acting like I missed him. But how exactly was I supposed to act? He left me when I needed him the most and he had traded me in for Reagan. Reagan! That hurt.

I had needed him, and he wasn't there. Now I knew that was because he was with her the whole time I was stuck in bed, lonely. How could he do that to me? I had to keep reminding myself that I was not who I used to be; that I needed to move on. The injury had made sure of that. There was a lot I was still going through, and I felt like I had no control over my body. The only way to regain control was to change my body, to tame and tone and make it submit to my will. So I pushed myself in exercise and eating, or, I should say, lack of eating. I could control what I put in my mouth, and I could control the number of steps I took. There was one more thing I needed to be in control of, and that was this situation. I needed to push him out of my mind. I needed to move on. Two years of hoping he'd call was enough.

When Mr. Parson finally got around to assigning our first writing project, my heart started racing. He asked us to write a memoir of an important moment in our life for homework. I couldn't do it. I just couldn't. I wasn't ready for a memoir. The only thing worth writing about was the actual accident. I couldn't do that. I wasn't ready to talk about it. I had to relive it every night in my dreams; I certainly didn't want to write about it. I wasn't paying close attention as he taught us about memoirs and how to write them. I was trying to make myself stop shaking. I looked at the clock. Ten, ten more minutes.

It became hard to breathe.

I tried to think: *How long can a person live without oxygen?*

My heart was racing.

My hands shook.

My vision started to dim.

Class wasn't over yet, but I had to go immediately. I fumbled with my bag. Damn it! Where was the guidance counselor's note saying I could leave class? I couldn't find it. Papers spilled everywhere. It was bright orange, but I couldn't find it. Someone shoved a paper in my hand. The note! "Go," Marco said, but I was already charging to the front of the room. I thrust the note in Mr. Parson's face without saying a word. Then I turned and smashed through the door.

The last thing I heard was Reagan laughing. The hallway smelled like old shoes and meatloaf, but at least I was free. I started to breathe again, just a little. Short, fast breaths. Then I heard them, footsteps. Someone was following me. Why were they following me? My breath caught. I ran.

"Larkin! LARKIN!"

I kept running.

"Larkin, please stop." Luke caught up to me, grabbed my arm, and pulled me tight. I was trapped! He trapped me. His arms were a snare at the bottom of the abyss.

No!

I pushed against him, but I couldn't break free. Why did he follow me? Why was he holding me? My heart felt like it was going to explode.

"Let me GO!"

"No, Larkin, I'm trying to help you."

I gained some sort of superhuman strength, broke his grasp, and punched him in the nose. He grabbed at his face; bright red blood was seeping out through his fingers. I turned and ran down the hall.

"Damn it, Larkin!" he yelled.

When I got to the guidance office, I collapsed. All I was asked to do was write a paper. I could have even made up a story, anything. He wouldn't have known if it was fake or not, but I wasn't thinking clearly. Here I had thought I was doing so well, but I wasn't. I should have never walked into the building this morning. Instead, I sat in the guidance lobby with my head in my hands, weeping.

Everyone, and I mean everyone, was going to hear about what happened. I would never live it down. I lifted my head for a moment. There they were, Luke and Reagan. She was holding a tissue box and he was holding red bloody tissues to his nose. She had her arm around his back as if trying to guide him. I tried to shrink down as small as I could so they couldn't see me.

Luckily, they got past without noticing me at all, heading for the nurse's office.

Dr. Smith came out of her office, took one look at me, came over, and knelt down in front of me.

"Are you okay?" she asked.

"No, not at all," I sobbed.

"Come on, come into my office. Take a moment to get it out."

She led me to her office where I flopped down onto her bright red couch.

"I have to get to a meeting, but you are welcome to stay here for a bit, okay?"

I was relieved that I could just sit in silence, "Thank you."

Mrs. Smith left, and I sat cradled by her huge, overstuffed couch. It was soothing, warm, and welcoming. I wanted to just stay there forever, hiding. I worked on my breathing the way the doctors had taught me. For once, they actually helped. I could feel my vision slowly focus again and my heartrate start to slow down. I knew I couldn't continue freaking out like that, but I had no idea how to stop it. Once a panic attack started, I lost all control.

I watched the minutes tick by on Mrs. Smith's wall clock. After a half hour, I decided to go home for the day. I resigned myself to the fact that coming back for my senior year was a spectacular mistake. My mother had known this would happen. I thought I was strong enough. But I wasn't. At that moment, I was definitely weak. I had let myself down. Something had to change.

"Larkin?" Mr. Parson's voice broke my chain of thought. He must have left his class. "I'm really concerned for you." He came and sat down next to me. His eyebrows furrowed. "What happened back there. Was that a panic attack?"

"Mr. Parson . . . "

"Call me Paul."

"Okay, Paul." I took a breath before starting. "I get into certain situations and my body feels like it's going to explode. They say I'm having serious panic attacks, but it really feels like I'm dying or something," I said, wringing my hands together. "When you brought up the memoir, I just couldn't handle it." I stopped talking, then took a breath. "My body acted on its own and I ran."

"What is it about the assignment?" Mr. Parson asked. *Weird*. I was sure he was getting updates from my dad the whole time.

"I don't want to write about the accident, but it's what everyone wants to hear about, over and over and over again. I'm sick of talking about it." I fiddled with my bag. "Then after that everything is boring. It's just me lying in darkness, reading books, and going to doctor appointments. There's nothing to write about. I don't want to write about my life before the accident, because everything changed." I shrugged and ran my hands through my hair. "I've changed. I've changed and I don't want to write about it."

"I understand." Mr. Parson said. "You are grieving your old life. Maybe writing about the accident would help you to work through it all?"

"I don't know if I'm ready for it." Tears welled up in my eyes, but I stayed calm and took a deep breath.

"Why don't you try writing the first paragraph, and we'll see how it goes," he said, looking pensively at me. "If you can't do it after trying, then write about something else."

"Okay, I can try." I said what he wanted to hear. What choice did I have? I didn't want to write about it. I just wanted it to go away. I wanted to be normal again. The last thing I wanted was to dwell on it.

"If you need to leave class again, it's okay. Just try not to punch other people, okay?"

Oh crap! I had momentarily forgotten I had punched Luke.

"It's okay, he was probably deserving anyway," Mr. Parson chuckled.

Honestly? It was a badass move, even if I wasn't in complete control.

"Yeah," I nodded. "That was a high point to my panic attack." We both laughed at my attempt to make light of the situation.

"Okay. I'm going to head down to the principal's office and let him know exactly what happened. I need to get in there before Luke does. He really shouldn't have grabbed you like that, although, I understand why he did. You need to realize that he thought hugging you would calm you down."

Whatever.

"He had no idea that that would be a horrible thing for someone in the middle of a panic attack. Lesson learned for him," he said.

I nodded.

I was calming down, but my headache was starting to spike. After experiencing two panic attacks in one day, I really needed to go home. I should have just gone to the nurse's office, but Luke was there. I decided to just leave.

. 8 .

Reagan

"I don't know what you were thinking," I snapped at Luke.

His face was smeared with blood and the tissue in his hand was bright red. I handed him another.

"I mean seriously. She's insane. You know that, right? She is insane."

"Just shut up," he snapped. His voice was muffled and nasally. His nose was obviously swelling on the inside. "This is not helpful right now."

"Sorry, I just don't understand. That wasn't normal."

"Yeah, no shit. Just shut up," He snapped, again, louder.

We kept walking in silence down an almost empty hallway. People stared. I mean, who wouldn't stare. His face was covered in blood.

"Do you think it's broken?" I asked in a small voice.

"I said, SHUT UP."

He may have been yelling at me, but I was happy. I really thought the Larkin issue would go away and he would stop staring at her. There was no way he would still be interested in her after she punched him. I wondered though, had she always been this violent?

I needed to help him down the steps to the lower level where the nurse's office was located. I held on to his arm to guide him, one step at a time. With each step, he became more and more angry.

We found our way to the nurse. She jumped out from behind her desk when she saw him, which wasn't surprising. He looked like a horror show.

"What happened?" She said, rushing towards us. She took hold of his arm and sat him down to look at him.

I started speaking, "Well, Lar . . . " He cut me off.

"Could you just let me tell my own story for once?"

I sat down in a chair on the other side of the bright, sterile room and watched as he said what happened.

"Larkin Phillips got upset and ran from the classroom."

"What classroom?" the nurse asked.

"Mr. Parson's Creative Writing."

"Go on."

"So, I left the room, running after her. I wanted to calm her down. When I reached her she seemed like she couldn't breathe."

"Okay." She said that in such a way that made me believe she already knew what happened next.

"I tried to hug her, to calm her down."

The nurse sighed. "Okay. I understand. Let's get you fixed up. I want to make sure nothing is broken."

She went to get a wet cloth to clean his face and an ice pack, then came back.

"Once you're cleaned up, we'll get some ice on that. Okay?" She began wiping the blood off his cheeks, then got out a small flashlight to look in his nose. She pushed on his face.

"It doesn't seem like anything is broken, but I want you to just hang out here for a little bit, just to make sure the bleeding stops." She handed him the ice. "Let's keep this ice on it for a bit." Then she turned to me, "Reagan, you should probably go back to class. I can take it from here."

"But . . ."

"Reagan, there's nothing you can do. Go back to class. You can connect with him later."

"Okay."

I got out of my chair and walked to him. I wanted to give him a hug or something, but when I got there, he looked at me, looked away, then said, "No. Just go."

I left.

I'm the one that helped him, but then he acted out against me. *WTF?!* I didn't understand.

.9.

Larkin

No one was there when I got home, which was perfect. I had about two hours to get a nap until my brothers got home to wreak havoc. I put my backpack by the door and went upstairs to the bedroom I had spent the last few years in. It was particularly bright in my room, so I pulled down my blackout blinds and collapsed on the bed. It felt so good to feel my head sink into my pillow. My eyes were closed for only 15 minutes when my cell phone alerted me that I had a text, the light from the phone made headache worse. I looked down and of course . . . it was Reagan.

***

Reagan: U really hurt Luke, I thought you should know. >:(

***

She literally stood there watching and laughing the entire time. I decided not to deal with it. I was too tired for anything she was going to spew my way.

Wrapped in my favorite Amish quilt and snuggled up with Vivi, my stuffed elephant, I drifted off to sleep.

My little brother's jarring scream woke me. "I got you. I shot you! You have to play dead!" cried Adam.

"No! That's not the rules! You can't just make up your own rules!" yelled John, my littlest brother.

"Haha, I can too," replied Adam in a smug voice.

I heard the stomp of a foot. John was mad and about to throw a tantrum. "I'm not playing anymore. You're a cheater!" he screamed.

The stomp came in my room.

"Sissy, are you up yet?" John whispered in my ear. "Sissy . . . Sissy, will you come play nerf guns with me? Adam cheats."

"Okay." I turned my face and gave him a kiss on his wet tear stained cheek. "Give me a few minutes to get out of bed." John was eight years old and the kindest boy, until he got mad, then he'd bum rush you. The kid could be brutal.

"Okay. Sissy?" he asked in the sweetest little voice.

"Yes?"

"Sissy, did you beat up someone today?" His eyes were wide.

"Yep," I replied, feeling shame instantly. What a great role model I was.

"NO WAY!!!" He gave me a fist bump before running out of the room, yelling for Adam to tell him that I "kicked someone's butt." How quickly he forgot that he was mad at Adam.

I got out of bed slowly and tried to fight my dizziness. I steadied myself and found a Nerf rifle in front of my door. Well, of course I was going to win. He left me the best gun we had! I quietly snuck towards John's doorway, where he had already forgotten our scheduled battle. As he picked up his Lego action figure, I aimed and shot him right in the forehead. He was shocked, but started to laugh, which then turned into a cry. I felt a little guilty, but I couldn't help but laugh. That's when he really got mad, turned red, and ran up to me. Before he could kick me, I grabbed him in a tight hug. I wanted to show him how much I loved him and what a great kid I thought he was.

While I was hugging him, I realized that was why Luke had grabbed me and was trying to hold me. He had grabbed me because he cared. I mean, obviously, he was trying to calm me down, but was it more than that? I mean, he even did it while his girlfriend watched. I had a lot to think about.

"I'm sorry, John."

"It's okay, Sissy. Actually, it was kind of funny." We started laughing together.

We laughed until our sides hurt. But I had to stop, I had to face my mom. I walked down the steps toward the kitchen. When I entered, she was standing over the stove throwing penne in a pot of boiling water, and my dad was at our island cutting up salad greens. They both stopped what they were doing and came over to me to hug me. That was my clue that they had heard from the school.

"Sweetie, Paul called earlier," Mom said as she touched my arm gently. "He said he took care of the situation and you have nothing to worry about with the school."

I was right. She knew everything. This was a major drawback to having a family friend as a teacher.

"What happened?" Dad asked. I thought I was going to be yelled at, but his eyes were sympathetic.

"I was in the middle of a panic attack, and he grabbed me and . . ." I stopped talking for a moment, trying to figure out what to say, "It was like a reflex; I couldn't stop it." I paused to look at my mom. She looked scared.

"What caused you to have a panic attack?" she asked. I found it interesting that she didn't already know that.

Tears welled up in my eyes while I told my mom what had happened during English class, "I started thinking about writing what happened during that game, and it just set off a panic attack." I felt my heart rate start to rise again. "My first reaction was to run out of the room. My legs just started moving on their own, and there was nothing I could do about it." I was speaking quickly.

My mother hugged me, making me feel safe. My dad paced around the kitchen, making me feel nervous. "I don't think I'm ready to go back. I think I just need to be homeschooled."

"Let's sit down and chat," my dad suggested.

I knew I wasn't going to get my way; I knew he was going to make me finish the year.

"Larkin, you have to realize that we need to find a way to make these panic attacks stop. We really think the more used to being in groups of people, the better prepared you will be in the future. It gives you a chance to work on coping mechanisms."

"Are you serious? That's not how it works!" I snapped at him.

"We're going to make an appointment with Dr. Eli. We need to talk to him about different options for you," my dad replied. Dr. Eli was my psychologist. "Larkin, you are so intelligent, you need every opportunity you can possibly get. Our school district is one of the best in the area."

"And there is nothing better than having a personal tutor." I was really trying to change his mind.

"Larkin, there was no way we could afford that on our own. You know the school district paid for that because you had medical reasons keeping you from school."

"And panic attacks are not considered a medical reason?" I asked.

"They are. But let's just see if it gets better. Keep at it a little while longer, and we'll make a decision a month from now. Okay?"

"This is a mistake; you have no idea how hard this is for me." I was pleading.

"I'm sorry honey, but sometimes the best thing to do is the hardest."
GAH!!!!

I wanted to say so much more, but it had been a really long day. Plus, I really didn't feel like having my headache spike again. It just wasn't worth it to argue. They'd have gotten what they wanted anyway.

"Fine, I'm going back to my room," I said as I turned and started to stomp up the stairs. I knew exactly how immature I was being, but I didn't care.

"But, honey, it's almost time to eat. Come back and help us set the table," my mom called after me.

Food. It was always food. I didn't want to eat. When I looked in the mirror, I no longer saw the toned muscular athlete. I looked awful. I didn't want to put food in my mouth. Why didn't anyone understand that? I wanted to feel better AND look better, and I was going to do it my way.

"I'm not hungry," I shouted back.

I hadn't run that day, so there was no way I was going to eat pasta. There was no way I was putting any calories into my body. On my way up the steps, I could hear my parents whispering again. I always hated that feeling. The one where people talk about you as if you aren't actually there. It felt disrespectful. They had no idea what was going on in my mind or how hard today had been. All of this felt like punishment. Whether they meant to or not, they were punishing me. It wasn't fair.

I stopped in Adam's room and peeked in. He was 13-years-old and, I surmised, the most popular boy in the whole middle school world. He was Facetiming one of his many girlfriends. This kid blew my mind. He was a little short for his age, but he had brown eyes with freakishly long lashes, and the most amazing curly dirty blond hair. He knew he had been slaying the girls since he was a baby. Knew it and used it. I was scared of what he might become in high school.

I leaned against his door frame. "Hey bub," I said quietly.

"Hey, Lark, did today go okay?"

"I think you already know. Not well."

"I was just trying to be nice," he said with a shrug. "Sorry, tomorrow will be better."

"I doubt it. Am I on mute?"

"Nope."

"Hi Ally!" I yelled.

"Seriously, Lark? I'm talking to Ashley!" He looked mad. He got up and walked with his hand held up, ready to push me out the door. "Out!

Go! Get out!"

In the background I heard Ashley say, "What? You talk to Ally? What the hell!"

"Oops, sorry. Bye." I laughed. I enjoyed doing that to him. I knew it was Ashely. I mean, what good were little brothers if you couldn't pick on them?

"Bye and try not to ruin my life next time." He slammed the door. No matter what, my brothers were always fun to torture. The door opened back up. He came out and hugged me tightly. "Larkin, I'm so glad you are living again."

I went back to my room and stared at myself in the mirror, trying hard to force myself to become stronger.

"You can do this. You are strong!" I said to my mirror-self. But all I saw was a fat round face and a tangled mess of brown hair that no one would ever take seriously. I hated the way I looked.

As if she knew my inner thoughts, my mom knocked on the door. "I brought you dinner."

"Actually, mom, I was going to change and go out for a run."

"Larkin, you are beautiful. You don't need to run right now. You need to eat."

"Mom, I didn't exercise for two years and I became huge."

"Look at yourself. Really look at yourself." She stood behind me looking in the mirror with me. "You are absolutely beautiful. Larkin, you had a serious injury. There are parts of your brain that were damaged, but your brain is working hard at rewiring everything," she said, smoothing my hair. "That's the only reason you think you are overweight."

I rolled my eyes.

"No, don't roll your eyes at that, it's true . . . " I began listening, "but, Larkin, you are so underweight that it's becoming dangerous. I love you so much. I don't want to see you do this to yourself," she said wiping her eye. My mother was always emotional. Then, after everything that happened the past two years, she started worrying even more. "Do you think maybe your panic attacks would be easier to deal with if you weren't hungry all the time?"

"Mom, that's what you don't understand. I'm never hungry. I hate the way food feels in my stomach."

"Think of food as medicine, darling. No one likes to take medicine, but sometimes we have to. You may not want to eat, but you have to. Your brain needs all the good stuff that's in food."

"I know, Mom. I know I need to do this. I know I need to eat." I tried to say anything to get her off my back.

"How was your headache today?"

"It was only a three out of ten for most of the day."

"Did it go higher?"

"Yeah, after one of my anxiety attacks."

"Do you need an appointment with your neurologist?"

"If they get worse, yeah."

My mom stuck around, probably to watch me eat. She did that often, but she always disguised it as wanting to hear about my day. While we talked, I counted the calories I put in my mouth. We talked about the two panic attacks and how I could have handled them better. She helped me to see that I did have some good moments and reminded me to think about those times. We laugh about how I punched Luke in the face. Honestly though, I was actually starting to feel bad about that.

Once my mom was gone, I decided to text Luke. I needed to apologize to him, to explain myself. He didn't have a clue as to what was going on and that wasn't fair to him.

***

Larkin: Luke, I'm so sorry for punching you

Luke: What's going on with u, Lark? Can I come over to talk?

***

A wave of heat rushed over me. I felt like I owed him a real conversation, but I wasn't looking forward to it. I realized that explaining everything to him might help me. Maybe I could find out why he had forgotten about me. My emotions were all over the place.

***

Larkin: Okay, sure. Come over.

***

I ran downstairs to let my parents know. "Mom, Luke is coming over to talk about what happened today."

"Are you sure that's a good idea?" She looked concerned.

"I have to see him every day, so I need to make sure things aren't weird. I need to apologize and explain everything." I felt like I was trying to convince them as much as I was hoping to convince myself.

"Okay, we'll be right here, just in case you need us." She said that as if he was the one who was dangerous, but really, it was me that was the problem.

"It'll be fine, Mom."

. 10 .

Reagan

My mom's car was in the driveway when I got home. I needed to tell her what was going on. Luke's dad's company used my mom's law firm often, so if something was wrong, she needed to know. I decided to just go in and get the conversation over with as quickly as possible.

As I walked up the walkway to my house, I stopped to look at my neighbors who were cutting or watering their lawns. I could hear the laughter of small children playing at the daycare down the street. I wanted to be a small kid again. That sort of laughter doesn't happen anymore. It felt like there was a huge weight over me. If my relationship with Luke ended badly, it would look bad for my mother. I knew that.

I opened the heavy oak front door and a blast of cool air hit me in the face. I could hear my mother's voice on a phone call from her study. She never liked being interrupted, so I quietly walked up the steps to my room, closed the door, and sat on my bed with my phone in my hand, texting.

***

Reagan:	Are you okay?
Luke:	Yeah
Reagan:	Can I come over later?
Luke:	No, I have stuff to do
Reagan:	Love you

***

I waited for him to say it back, but he didn't. I felt like I was going to puke. How could I lose him to someone that was so obviously violent? That's when my door flew open.

"How was your first day?" my mom asked.

"Okay."

"Good," she said and turned to leave the room.

That was when I added in, "Larkin is back."

She turned back around. "What now?"

"She's back, Mom."

"Okay, well, she's a nobody now. It's not like she's going to get on the team again or anything."

"Right, well, she punched Luke in the nose, and I think he loves her again."

"Excuse me?"

"She pun . . ."

"I heard you. Go back to the part about him loving her?"

"He's distant."

"You cannot let her get him back. He is yours."

"Mom, I don't own him."

"No, but we . . . you need him."

I sighed then said, "I'll do what I need to do."

"That's right, you will. WHATEVER you need to do. Dress like you care tomorrow, okay?" She turned again to leave the room, "Oh, and Reagan, don't mess this up like you do everything else."

I buried my face in my pillow and began to scream. I was sure she heard me, but I was equally sure she didn't care. More and more anger welled up inside of me. I needed to get it out. I got up, flung my door open, ran down the steps, threw on my slides, and ran out the front door. Luke had told me he didn't want to hang out, but I didn't care, I was going to his house.

I was so enraged; I don't even remember walking there. Somehow, I ended up at his house. His car wasn't there, but I walked up the driveway anyway, paying attention to nothing but my rage. I turned onto the sidewalk to his front door. On the way there, something scratched me on my arm. I hadn't realized I had veered off the path, making my arm run against his mother's rose bush. I ripped off a rose and threw it on the ground, then kept walking. I stepped up onto his porch where I could hear someone playing a piano. I pounded on the door as loudly as I could, then rang the doorbell a few times. Luke's mother answered the door.

"Reagan, honey, what's wrong? You look awful." Then she looked me over and noticed that my forearm was bleeding from the rose thorn. "You are bleeding a little. Come in, we can wash it and get you some ointment."

I didn't budge I didn't care about the dumb scratch, "Is Luke here?"

"No. I'm not sure where he is."

"Is he at Larkin's?"

"Larkin's? That's a name I haven't heard in a while," she said.

I just turned around and walked away, trying to hold back my tears. I knew where he was.

He was under her spell, even after she punched him. I knew it.

. 11 .

Larkin

Luke lived right around the corner, so it didn't take much time for him to be standing in front of me, swollen nose and all.

"Oh Luke, I am so sorry." I threw my arms around him to hug him as tears welled up in my eyes. I instantly started worrying that I had given him a concussion. I rattled off questions, as if I was a living checklist. "Luke, look at me." I held up two fingers, "How many fingers am I holding up."

"Two. Larkin, you don't have to do this."

"Just shut up. Close your eyes and try to stand straight," I demanded. He was able to do that just fine.

"With a concussion, you will sometimes get dizzy and fall over," I explained.

"Lark, really, I'm fine."

"What's the date?" I asked pensively.

"Oh my God, Larkin. It's Monday, August 31st."

"Who was the first President."

"Washington."

"Do you remember how you got hurt?"

"Um, yeah, you punched me in the face," he said, looking at me as if I had lost my mind.

"Right."

I didn't want to piss him off more than I already had, so I stopped.

"The doctor didn't say anything about a concussion?" I looked him straight in the eyes as I asked.

I had forgotten how beautiful his eyes were. I could feel myself falling under his spell, but that was a spell I wanted no part of.

"No concussion. They did the same checks you just did and more. Oh yeah, you also didn't successfully break my nose, so you might want to try harder in the future," he said with a sly grin. "So, uh, you wanna tell me what's going on with you? Maybe?" As he spoke, he looked down at the ground, then back up with his eyes. Shivers.

I took a deep breath. I wasn't sure where to start, and I wasn't exactly sure if I could trust him. He pretty much . . . put me out to pasture when I was injured.

"I would never hurt you intentionally."

"Okay, so spill?" he demanded.

"I'm doing well with the physical part of my head injury, but there are some things that still need work," I said, then took a deep breath, getting ready to talk about really personal things. "I have these panic attacks where I become overwhelmed and anxious about everything. I try to control it, but I really can't."

Luke listened to me intently as I spoke.

"It's all a mess. But I am seeing a therapist and we are working on it."

We sat down on my porch swing. He angled himself toward me and put his hand on my knee. Complete butterflies. I tried to get control because I knew he wasn't worth it.

"So, what happened with the injury? You just sort of fell off the face of the earth. No one knew what to think and we really didn't know what to do," he said. He looked at me with furrowed brows. What he said made me mad, and he could tell. "Tell me what's going on. I'm missing something here," he said quickly.

"You're missing something? I missed something! I missed my life! I missed my friends! Everyone forgot about me," I snapped. I was beginning to get emotional, a tear dropped down to my cheek. I quickly wiped it away before he could notice.

"No, no, no, we didn't forget you. I promise you, we didn't. We just didn't know what to do."

"It's simple; you check in on me."

"We were told that you couldn't look at your screen to text. We would call, and your mom would say you were sleeping. None of us were driving then, so we couldn't pop by. Then, after a while, we didn't know what else to do," he pleaded.

Let's just ignore the fact that he lived within walking distance.

"It wasn't like that forever. For the first five months I couldn't look at screens. The light would hurt my eyes. And, yeah, I did sleep a lot. That's what I was supposed to do, but it wasn't all the time, and it wasn't every day."

"Larkin, we were all scared. Remember, we were younger, and we didn't understand what had happened."

"Imagine how I felt. I don't get it. You all forgot about me."

"We didn't, I promise." He looked into my eyes again. "Baby, I could never forget about you, or replace you, or any of those things." He stroked my cheek with his fingers.

"But you did replace me. You started dating Reagan," I replied. *I mean, honestly, he could never replace me? Why did I ever fall for him?* "I thought you loved me," I said in a small voice.

"I did, and I do. Reagan just sort of . . . happened."

"Happened?" I couldn't believe he used such nonchalant terms as . . . *just sort of happened.*

"Before we talk about that, can we focus on what's been going on with you for the past two years?" he said.

I sighed. I felt like I always had to talk about that, over and over again. At each new doctor's appointment. Every time we ran into someone at the grocery store. At church! But I realized I really did need to talk to Luke about it and I realized it was important to do.

"It was just really hard. You were there. You remember what happened, right?"

"Oh yeah, I saw the whole thing. Getting kicked in the back of your head, then your head bouncing off the goal post. There was so much blood. When they came on the field and carried you off on a stretcher, I was scared out of my mind." He sounded like a sports announcer relaying what happened. I wasn't awake for a lot of what he was recounting, so I stopped listening. *Seriously, why was he telling me what happened to ME?* I didn't want to be rude, but he wouldn't shut up.

Finally, I yelled, interrupting him, "Okay, look, I know exactly what happened to me, I don't need to relive it." The pressure was building, I had to get it out, "Obviously my accident left an impression on you. I'm sorry for that. I'm sorry for punching you. I'm sorry for all of it." I sat there apologizing to HIM, but he needed to apologize to ME!

At first, he took his arm back and backed away looking at me with his eyes wide and his mouth slightly open. He had no idea what to do or say. Then, he took a deep breath, put his arm back around my shoulder, and leaned in close.

He spoke slowly, "I'm so sorry, babe. That was stupid. Please forgive me." He stroked my shoulder. Then he leaned into my ear and whispered, "Please, let me make it up to you."

"No!" I batted his arm away and slid back. "I, I have to go in and do some reading . . . or something."

In one motion, I got up and ran into my house, swinging the front door open and slamming it shut behind me. I leaned against the door for a few moments to breathe, long and slow, trying to calm my nerves.

"Larkin, what's wrong?" My mother came running. She found me breathing loudly with my eyes closed.

"I'm okay." I pushed past her and rushed up the stairs to my room.

. 12 .

Reagan

Reagan: Where are you?

Luke: What?

Reagan: Where the hell are you?

Luke: No . . . "Hey, Luke, how's your nose?"

Reagan: No. Where are you?

Luke: I'm at home

Reagan: No, you aren't, I was just there

Luke: What the hell is wrong with you? Why are you being so possessive?

It doesn't look pretty on you.

Reagan: No, I'm not. I know you are with her.

Luke: With who?

Reagan: Larkin

Luke: No, I'm not. Seriously, I'm becoming offended by this line of accusations. I'm in my bedroom.

Reagan: I just talked to your mom. She said you weren't there.

Luke: Well, I was.

Reagan: Where was your car?

Luke: In the garage. Seriously, you are acting insane.

Reagan: Were you really there?

Luke: Yes. I've been in my room all night.

Reagan: Oh. I'm sorry, baby

Luke: You don't trust me. How can we have a relationship if you act jealous all the time?

Reagan: I'm so sorry. Please forgive me. Can I come over now and make it up to you?

Luke: No, not right now, I want to be alone.

Reagan: Babe, I love you.

Luke: I need some time.

***

Reagan: What the hell is wrong with you?

Larkin: Reagan, don't

Reagan: DON'T? How about DON'T punch my boyfriend in the face?!

Larkin: You don't understand.

Reagan: Oh, I understand. I understand ur a freak

Larkin: It was a panic attack

Reagan: Whatever

Larkin: Luke came by to talk about it, he was fine.

Reagan: He came over? To your house?

Larkin: Yeah, he's fine. So, calm down.

Reagan: WTH???!!!! He told me he was at home all night. You are lying.

Larkin: Oh, I'm sorry, you didn't know? Hmmmm

Reagan: Stay away from him!

Reagan: Freak!

Larkin: Reagan, it's not a big deal. Everything is fine

Reagan: STAY. AWAY. FROM. HIM!

. 13 .

Larkin

I needed to run, I had to get out of the house. I had to clear my mind. Luke was bad for me. But even though I knew that, I still planned on running past his house.

I stopped to catch my breath a little in front of his house. Deep in my soul I hoped he'd see me and come out. I stayed there for a while, but he never did come out. What were my feelings for him? I wasn't really sure. I kept telling myself he was just something familiar for me to hang onto, that was all, just familiar. But he dropped me and ended up with Reagan, of all people! Reagan! I needed to stay away from him, but there I was in front of his house. I was a mess.

The longer I stood there, the more furious I became at myself. Was I misreading him? There I was, restarting my life during my last year of high school, getting ready to work on college applications, and I was worrying about a boy? I needed to grow up and get ahold of myself!

I ran about three miles and it felt so good. It wasn't terribly hot out, but garden sprinklers were still running. Sometimes I ran through one shooting water over the sidewalk. As I ran, I tried to keep count of how many calories I burned. It helped me to keep going, even when fatigue set in. I loved this time by myself. I loved the pain, the burning, and the lost breath.

My house was always so loud. Running gave me time to sort out my thoughts. My mother said I obsessed over things; that I thought too much. But how else would I do better the next time? Being better, doing better was what I needed to do. So, I took things into my own hands. Running gave me a headache, of course, but I didn't care. I was so used to the headaches by then, a spike from a 3 to 5 level headache was worth it. The only thing that mattered was that running cleared my soul.

When I finished my run, I dashed into my house and up the stairs. My phone was beeping. Three friend requests. I didn't have many friends on social media. They were mostly just some of the other teens at physical therapy and a few from the homeschool group I would go to when I was feeling well enough, which wasn't that often. I spent so long not being able to look at screens that I had escaped the social media addiction thing. I laid down on my bed with my phone in hand. Before I checked my notifications, I had to check my Fitbit app to see how many calories I had burned. Around 500 calories. I could handle that!

Only after I closed my calorie counter, did I go to my friend requests. There were three: Luke, Brooke, and Marco. I wondered if Luke was thinking about me as I was running past his house. Maybe he saw me. Brooke was a given, of course she friended me. I think she missed me and was feeling badly that she hadn't made an effort to see me. Marco . . . the thought of him wanting to get in touch brought a smile to my face. With everything that happened it surprised me that I wasn't embarrassed to be near him, but for some reason I wasn't.

I clicked "Accept Request" on all three.

***

Brooke: Hey Grrl! So excited ur back!

Larkin: Thanks! <3 seeing you 2day.

Brooke: Can u play soccer again?

Larkin: No. :(

Brooke: :(Hey, having a back2school swim party at my house this weekend. U coming?

Larkin: Sure, send me the information.

Brooke: KK. Oh, also, I talked to Coach, he said he would love to you help with that team I told you about. He just needs a doctor's signature. He'll be in touch.

Larkin: I'm not sure I'm ready.

Brooke: Just talk to him and see what he says. They are little kids, you'll be safe.

Larkin: I need to think about it. See u tomorrow?

Brooke: Yep! I'm so glad you're back.

***

The thought of coaching kids sounded like fun. There was no way they could kick the ball high enough to hit my head and it wasn't like they would ever tackle me for the ball. I decided to seriously think about it.

Brooke's party concerned me more. Part of me jumped at the chance for a swimming party and to show Luke what he had been missing. The other part worried about how I looked. I thought maybe if I drank a lot of water to flush myself out, ate only greens with lemon juice, and ran before and after school it would help. I resigned myself to that plan.

I didn't even think I wanted Luke back. Or maybe I did. What I needed to do was to let Reagan have him. Let him alone and forget about it. I mean, honestly, how could I have ever thought about going back to someone who wasn't there for me when I needed him? Isn't that the whole point of a relationship, to have someone there for you? But it didn't matter; I couldn't stop thinking about him.

I couldn't stop thinking about our first kiss when we hiked up to Pole Steeple. He wrapped his arms around me at the very top. He looked into my eyes and bent down to place his lips gently on mine. The sensation of that kiss lasted for days. It was my first kiss. Our first kiss. I kept thinking about it over and over again. Something was wrong with me. It was wrong. It was time to let go. I needed to become someone new, to reinvent myself. I needed to take care of myself and worry less about him.

I kept trying to reason with myself that I didn't actually want him back. Luke was my first boyfriend. We started dating in 7th grade. At that point he was all I knew. I was never interested in anyone else. The only thing I really cared about besides him was sports. But I didn't have that anymore; I didn't have either.

<DING>

It was Marco. Suddenly I was thinking less about Luke.

***

Marco:	Hey! How's that knee? Did they apprehend the aggressor?
Larkin:	I think I'll survive. I have a super hero bandage on it. And no, I'm sad to report that he's still at large.
Marco:	I hope they find him. Personally though, I would have chosen a bandage with race cars on it. I'm a little disappointed in hearing that a super hero is protecting your knee.
Larkin:	I was hoping for hearts and rainbows, but with two brothers, what can you do. They'll never find the assailant; he'll go on to skin another unsuspecting knee.
Marco:	It's not every day that a beautiful girl runs into me. To start my day like that? That's the stuff my dreams are made of.
Larkin:	Ha, funny!
Marco:	It's the truth.
Larkin:	Awe. Just a warning, I'm as crazy as they come. :P

Marco:	*"One must still have chaos in oneself to be able to give birth to a dancing star."*
Larkin:	Nietzsche.
Marco:	I have to say, I'm impressed. I mean, when you ran into me, I thought, "who is this beautiful klutz?"
Larkin:	Now THAT'S more like the truth.
Marco:	It's not though. Sometimes the clumsiest people are the smartest people.
Larkin:	How so?
Marco:	Clumsy people have more to worry about than running into people in a doorway. You're one of those people. You're impressive. Where did you come from? I don't remember you from last year.
Larkin:	I was injured and out of school for two years. I'm back now, but I don't really want to talk about that. Why don't I remember you from 9th?
Marco:	I moved here last year.
Larkin:	From where?
Marco:	Oh, out of state. Promise to run into me tomorrow? I have some papers that need damaging.
Larkin:	You think you're a funny guy? I'll try saying hi, instead of running into you.
Marco:	I'm not going to lie. I'm perfectly fine with you running into me.
Larkin:	Oh no, I would rather just say hello, it's a lot less messy.
Marco:	I think we might have a lot in common, let's make sure to chat again.
Larkin	Maybe we do. Good night.
Marco:	Fare thee well.

***

He barely knew me, but he still checked on me. If that same scene had happened with someone like Luke, he would call the girl a spaz and go on with his life.

. 14 .

Reagan

All I could think about was making sure Luke noticed me. I needed to look perfect, act perfect, BE perfect. I had to keep him at all costs.

What 17-year-old guy doesn't react to a girl throwing themselves at him? What the hell?

I began using my mom's foundation. That was not something I normally did, but I had to do something different. Nothing could be out of place, not one red splotch could show through. I applied concealer, just a shade lighter than my skin tone, making sure to put a line of it down the front of my nose for highlighting purposes. I buffed, then contoured. I had never done that on my own, but a woman at the make-up counter at Macy's did it for me once. When she did it, I looked like I weighed at least ten pounds less. That was what I needed, the illusion. Sucking in my cheeks, I put the brown color under my cheek bones. It was too dark. Good thing I wasn't working at Macy's, the customers would hate me. I hated me.

My stomach clenched as I bent over the sink to wash my face and start over. I lifted my head quickly, looked at myself, and breathed in deeply.

I told myself I could do this.

I had spent my life as an athlete. I only cared about sports, so I really had no clue what I was doing. Makeup was never a priority for me. Some girls seemed like they just knew how to be feminine. I didn't, but man, I was trying to learn. After quickly drying my face, I remembered something my mom told me. "Eyes first! Always do the eyes first!" Right! I grabbed my mom's YSL palette and a brush and swiped a light shade on my entire lid. Then I grabbed a darker shade for my lower top lid.

But that wasn't enough, I needed to be hot. Irresistible.

Then, I did the very thing I never thought I would. I picked up my mom's eyeliner marker, black. I took a deep breath as I removed off the cap.

I kept telling myself I could do this. *I mean, honestly, how hard could it be?*

My hands were shaking, so I clasped them together to get them to stop. Then, I brought the eyeliner marker to my right eyelid and began to trace my top lash line. *So far so good!* Then I swept out past the outer corner of my eye and blinked at the wrong time. I looked at myself in the mirror. It looked like I had been punched. I quickly washed it off before it dried and started the process over. The next time my hand shook in the middle of my eyelid and I poked myself in the eye. My eyes started to water.

I suddenly found myself with more respect for the girls at school with perfect cat eyes.

I decided to forgo the eye makeup all together. *Forget it! Just swipe some blush on my cheeks and use a small amount of translucent powder. You can do this!* Mission accomplished, I returned to my eyes and decided to go a little further. I swiped some mascara on my top lashes. Thankfully, I didn't poke myself in the eye again.

Instead of putting my hair up, I left it down and used some of my mom's gel to make it shine. Surprisingly, that worked well. *Last step, kissability.* A quick fix of my mom's Mac Matte Lipstick in Whirl on my lips completed my transformation. Before leaving my mom's room I stopped to take one last look in her full body mirror.

Okay, maybe I couldn't rock the eyeliner, but I could rock the lipstick! My skirt looked good; my tight pink shirt looked perfect. I felt drool worthy.

Feeling confident, I winked at myself.

I felt hot!

I turned to leave my mom's bathroom. If she had known I was in there, she would have killed me. My mom liked her privacy and didn't want me intruding or using her make-up, her clothes, or basically touching anything that was hers.

My pocket started to vibrate.

***

Luke: Here
Reagan: K babe

***

I ran down the steps, slipped on my ballerina flats that were next to the door, threw my backpack over my shoulder, and headed out the door. He was sitting in his jeep looking at me weirdly.

"Crap! Do we have a speech due today?" Luke asked as I climbed into his car.

"No. Why?" I asked.

"Well, you look like . . . that," he said as he looked me over from top to bottom. "You only dress up when you have to. So, what am I forgetting?"

He didn't compliment me. He just looked angry. He didn't see me; he didn't see the effort I put into how I looked that morning. The effort I put into looking nice for him.

"Well, thank you for that compliment." I rolled my eyes, closed the door, and stared out the window.

I kept telling myself not to cry. It wasn't sexy to cry, especially not with mascara on. He just didn't understand. I told myself all that, but really? It hurt to feel unseen.

I took a deep breath and turned to stare straight ahead.

In my mind, I was trying to will Luke to say something nice. Anything nice!

"You wanna come over tonight? My mom's out of town for a few days," I asked.

"Yeah, okay. Maybe," he shrugged.

"Right, okay. I was just thinking it's been a while."

There was silence. Dead silence. Not even the radio was on. Nothingness.

"A while for what?"

"Never mind. Just try."

Luke shrugged again. "Okay. I might be tired after practice though." I nodded. "Yeah, me too," I said, giving up.

"Did you hear back about your scholarship?" I asked, trying to think of something to say.

"No."

We both looked out the window without saying a word before I tried to start a conversation again.

"Anything good happening right now?"

"No."

"I like that shirt on you. You look good in royal blue." I kept trying.

"Yeah."

"Do you think I look nice today? I went a little extra."

"I guess," he said, staring straight ahead, both hands on the steering wheel.

He didn't notice me. He didn't notice everything I had done to make myself look better for him, to make him want me more. He didn't see me at all. I took a breath, "You feel a million miles away."

He sighed but continued to look straight ahead. My body heat rose, and not in a good way. I was becoming angry.

"Luke, what's going on?"

"Honestly, Reagan, why do you make everything into a big deal. I just have a lot on my mind," he answered.

"Luke, you have never turned me down. Not once."

"Reagan, it's okay." He grabbed my hand, but still wasn't looking at me.

"It's not okay. What's going on?"

"Nothing."

"Where'd you go last night?" I already knew the answer.

"Nowhere. Don't worry about it."

The only thing going through my mind were my mother's words. *You have to keep him. At all costs. You're nothing without him.*

"Well, I am worrying about it."

"Whatever."

I always hated it when he would do that, say, "whatever."

I stared at him harder.

"DO NOT DISMISS ME!" I snapped. I probably shouldn't have done that.

He said nothing, just stared straight ahead. That was what he always did, he would shut down when he was pissed. I knew I had really messed up when I snapped.

We pulled into school. Everyone was standing around waiting for the bell to ring. I could tell he was angry. I could see Izzy waiting for me by her car. He whipped into his spot, slammed on the breaks, and looked at me. His face was bright red. I saw Izzy watching. I hoped she didn't notice what was happening.

"Seriously? I'm not allowed to have a life? Do I HAVE to tell you everything?" he snapped at me.

"You went to HER house, didn't you?"

"Honestly, it's none of your business."

"Oh, but it is."

"Fine. You know what? Yes, I did."

"Right . . . Perfect." I turned to open the door of the Jeep.

He put his hand on my shoulder to stop me from getting out.

"No! Don't touch me," I snapped.

"Babe, I'm sorry. I just needed to talk to her about what happened."

"SHE PUNCHED YOU! What could you possibly have to talk about with her?"

"There's something going on. I needed to know . . ."

I cut him off before he could finish his sentence.

"She's back and she's messed up in the head now. What more could you possibly need to know?"

I turned away from him, took a breath, put on a fake smile, and stepped out of his Jeep. I absolutely could not let anyone know we had been fighting.

I stood in front of the Jeep waiting for him to get out. As he approached me, I gave him a cold look, grabbed his hand, and we started walking toward the school, smiling and nodding to our friends the whole time. The perfect couple.

. 15 .

Larkin

"Lark! Over here!" Brooke waved me over. "I'm so excited that we're finally in a class together."

"Hey Brooke!" I sat at the desk next to her.

"We really need to hang out again; I have so much to tell you," she said.

"We do, let's plan something!" I answered.

"Juice and Java after school today?"

I quickly thought about what I could safely order there, adding up calories in my head. I figured a cup of tea would be fine (zero calories).

"Don't you have soccer practice?" I asked.

"Nah, not this afternoon."

"Let's do it."

"So excited!" she smiled.

I had forgotten how much she made me laugh. I missed her. I really, really missed her. We'd been friends since Kiddie Kicker Kindy Soccer. I remember her being next to me on the field when a bee stung her. She screamed and started jumping up and down in pain. I ran up to her and held her as she cried until the coach could get to her. We'd been close ever since, until my accident.

Brooke looked up, a sly smile spreading across her face. "Luke, check it out! Lark is in this class with us."

He walked over and smiled at me. "Hmm, I'm not so sure I want to sit next to this slugger. She may kick my butt again." He started jumping around as if he were a boxer, laughed, then flopped in the desk in front of me and turned around.

"Hey babes, want to hang out tonight?" he looked me dead in the eyes. "The way we left things . . . I was really hoping we could talk more."

He touched my hand lightly, "What's up with you running off?"

Another proud moment. "I know. I'm sorry. I just can't sit and listen to what happened to me on that field. It's like a PTSD thing." He was looking into deeply into my eyes, listening to my every word. I could feel myself blush, but I continued, "You started to talk about the accident, and I needed to bolt." I hoped he actually cared and wasn't just going to use what I told him to spread rumors. I was also hoping he wouldn't tell everything I said to Reagan, who would, definitely, 100%, spread rumors.

"Look, I don't get what's going on." He moved his hand from my hand to my forearm, which gave me the chills. He took a moment to think, "I know we aren't together anymore, but you hold a serious part of my heart." He put his hands over his chest bone, "I'm here for you, babe."

The door flung open and the teacher came in. Luke quickly turned around. Mrs. Whitter was a squatty, pudgy woman with glasses and short salt and pepper hair. She was the most hilarious teacher we had. I tried to focus on her. But as the class laughed at her jokes, I just sat there staring at the back of Luke's head.

His scent brought back memories I had forgotten. We had been a great couple. Everyone thought so. Everyone also thought we'd be together forever. Sometimes things just don't work out the way we plan.

I smiled to myself, thinking about our trip to the lake. I remembered how we rented a two-person kayak. Luke thought he was so cool that he could stand up while we were in the kayak. Of course, we flipped. It was hysterical. We almost drowned because we were so busy laughing instead of treading water. I promised to never tell another soul about it. Later in the day we swam, jumped off the dive platform, and swung on the rope swing.

I remember nestling under a tree for a picnic lunch and holding hands whenever we could. It became hard to eat, because I really needed both hands. It was an amazing day. Remembering days like that that really made me miss Luke. I wondered if he took Reagan there to kayak. Did he take her to JoJo's after her games for pizza? Did he go to Rita's for Italian Ice after the movies? All of our special things, did he do them with her? I was paying more attention to my memories than I was to the history class.

I knew then that I could get him back. But did I want to? I honestly didn't know. All the warning signs were there, but I didn't see them. Part of me didn't want to see them. I just really needed someone I could trust, and he let me down. It was my senior year, I wanted to do well, get into college, and not to cause any drama. None of the bullshit was worth it. I mean, I knew we would all be leaving for college in less than a year anyway. What was the point? I didn't think I would be going to college with any of them. But still, I couldn't spend my senior year being angry and hiding from everyone.

I was shaken from my thoughts when a notebook was shoved onto my desk. That was how Brooke always communicated during class. We weren't allowed to have our cell phones out and notes would ALWAYS get the attention of a teacher. Passing notebooks made it look like we were sharing class information. So, while we were sharing personal notes, our teachers were proudly thinking that we were being extra studious.

"Do you want to invite Luke to Juice and Java? Girl, I see the way you are looking at him," she wrote.

Yes, it was THAT noticeable.

"No, I want bonding time with just you! I'm done with him."

"I wouldn't be so sure about that. Reagan is such a bitch. I think he was happier with you."

"Don't tell me that."

"<3"

Brooke always loved drawing hearts and flowers, so a handwritten heart emoji didn't surprise me at all.

I looked at her. She winked at me. I missed her so much. But I felt conflicted between being mad and being happy to just talk to her again.

I tried to listen to the last part of class. Good thing, too, otherwise I would have missed when Mrs. Whitter assigned our readings. The Fertile Crescent, easy enough. I noticed the time on the clock and put my hands over my ears. The bell didn't jar me at all when it rang. I remember it clearly because you remember those small victories, and for me that victory was when something didn't actually hurt. All the students gathered their stuff and got up to leave, including Brooke, who jumped up quickly.

"I'll see you at Juice and Java, kay?" Brooke reminded me before leaving the room.

Luke turned around in his seat, "Seriously, can we meet up?"

"Sorry, I'll be with Brooke. This gives you time to be with Reagan."

"Right, Reagan. Well, I definitely want to spend some time with you. Okay?"

"Maybe. We'll talk about it tomorrow." We walked out of the classroom together. He had his arm on my lower back which made it feel like old times. It also felt wrong.

"I have to run. Text me if you change your mind," he whispered to me. But before I could answer, he walked up to a freshman girl and leaned on the locker next to hers as she got her books out. She giggled and blushed at whatever he said.

That was when Reagan walked up to him, frustration in her eyes. She looked back and forth between Luke and the girl.

"Luke!" she snapped, looking pissed. She actually punched him in his side. He turned to her but seemed bothered that she was even there.

"Oh, hey." He grabbed her hand.

"You know what? Just don't," she snapped.

I was shocked. She actually caught him flirting. The only thing I could think at the time was to thank God that she didn't catch him with his arm around my back.

I walked away and decided not to watch. I didn't want to know what was going on. I had forgotten how much of a flirt he always was. I quickly got it out of my mind and told myself that I didn't need to worry about them. I had my own stuff to fret over.

I dodged into my next class, trying to clear my head. I plopped down at the desk next to Marco, who gave me a thoughtful look, "Better day?" he asked.

"Yeah, I think so." I flashed him a big toothy smile.

"Good." I snuck a look at him every once in a while, wondering where this was going. I mean, I had only just met him the day before, but already I felt comfortable with him. It really made no sense at all, but there it was. And, yes, he looked like a complete nerd, but damn it, there was just something about his eyes. The way they crinkled when he smiled at me.

After class he stuck around again. "So, what are you doing for lunch?"

"I'm not good with large crowds, so I'll probably just eat in the nurse's office," I said.

He looked shocked. "With the nurse?" he asked incredulously. "What if I can find some place quiet?"

"Um, sure? Where?" I asked.

"Why don't we eat out in the courtyard; not many go out there. I usually just sit there and play checkers or poker."

"Sounds good, but I'm not really into chess or poker," I answered sheepishly.

"How about talking? Are you into talking?"

That sounded like it might be a good idea. It would be quieter, and I could eat my apple and cottage cheese without someone harassing me to eat whatever mystery meat they were serving up. Plus, I wouldn't have to worry about Luke and Reagan.

"You know what? Yes, I absolutely love talking. I'll meet you there," I said with a wide smile.

It felt good. I felt like I was on a new path. Just saying yes set the course for something better. I could feel it.

. 16 .

Reagan

"Did you see that?" I asked Izzy.

"What?"

"He had his hand on her back," I replied.

"Who? What?" Izzy asked.

"Luke . . . Larkin!"

"Oh. What happened now?" Izzy asked lazily.

"He walked out of the classroom with his hand on her back!" I snapped.

"I think he's just worried about her."

"NO! He went to her house last night."

"WHAT?" Suddenly Izzy's posture became straight. She looked at me with wide eyes.

"Um, yeah. He went to her house."

"After she punched him? Is he nuts?"

"I don't know. She punches him, and he fawns over her. I tried to kiss him, and he pushed me away."

"Wait. He is pushing YOU away?"

"Yep," I nodded.

"Nope, time to go into bitch overdrive," Izzy replied with an attitude.

"I agree."

"Ruin her?"

"Ruin her," I replied.

Izzy and I walked our separate ways. If there was anyone I could always count on to have my back, it was Izzy. This was going to be good. I felt like I had a sense of purpose. I was taking control of the Larkin situation. If I could get enough people to doubt her, that would be enough.

I walked into Physics Lab and made my way to my lab group. I threw my backpack on the floor and flopped down into my seat. They were busy talking about Brooke's party.

"Reagan, you and Luke coming?" Sophie asked.

"Wouldn't miss it for the world," I replied. I looked around, "Hey, did you guys see what happened yesterday?"

"You mean," Leo looked at me with a smirk before going on, "Larkin going crazy on Luke? Who could have missed that?" Leo always had a flair for the dramatic.

"Yeah, what the hell was that?" I asked.

"I don't know, but it was some shit. Wasn't it?" said Sophie.

"Right?" I asked.

"Did you know she was doing MMA while she was out? Maybe she was hitting the gym hard," Leo added with a chuckle.

"No, I think she was too busy going completely mental," I added. "I knew she was out because of her head injury, but man, it feels like something else is going on." Everyone nodded. "I don't trust her being here. She's obviously unhinged."

"Honestly? It's kind of weird how she hides in the bathroom. Have you noticed that?" Sophie asked.

"How could I not?" I replied. "I mean, are we safe with her here?"

"I don't think she's violent or anything," Kate turned around to say.

"Are you serious? She PUNCHED Luke." I answered.

"True. But I don't know. I kind of feel bad for her." Kate replied.

"Seriously? Let me remind you, we were all there for her accident. Was it really that bad? I mean, seriously?" I was counting on the fact that none of them really remembered the accident. I knew what I was doing was wrong, but I didn't care. I had to do whatever I could.

"True. I mean, she was gone for two years! How could it have been that bad?" Kate remarked.

"I heard Danielle say she saw her at the mall a few times last year and she seemed completely fine," Sophie noted.

"Yeah, and I see her running all the time. That's not something someone with a head injury would do," Leo interjected.

"Right? I know some people with real brain damage. She can walk, she can run, and she can feed herself. I call bullshit," I replied.

It was actually working, I honestly didn't think it would, because she was the beloved Larkin. It's amazing how quickly people will turn on each other if nudged a little bit.

"Right, and sometimes she needs sunglasses and sometimes she doesn't," Leo remarked. "I'm calling bullshit too."

"She was probably just trying to get out of school," Sophie said.

"No, I heard she had a tutor, she was still doing schoolwork," Kate said, defending Larkin again. I made a mental note of it.

"Oh, come on, having a personal tutor? You know that was easier. Did she even have an injury that was that bad? I mean, I saw it happen, but she obviously milked it," Leo added.

"Yeah, and now she gets out of classes early if she fakes a panic attack. She's allowed to be late to classes so she can hide in the bathroom. She gets more time for tests. Basically, she's getting away with everything," I said.

"Wait, wait, wait. I saw her and Luke walking together. Are you upset just because of that? Are you jealous?" Kate said. She was really bothering me. I shot her a look, hoping she would realize that she needed to shut her mouth. She shot me the same look right back.

"Are you kidding? No. She punched him." I laughed a little, then said, "Trust me, I am not afraid of her taking Luke from me." I waved my right hand in a way to dismiss her.

"It's strange. I've never heard of a concussion patient needing YEARS," Leo said.

"That's true," Kate nodded.

"Yeah, it doesn't seem right. I'll be honest, I've never trusted her anyway. Her nice girl act? Whatever," Sophie added.

"The act should stop now. She's full of shit," I replied, knowing I had won them. I felt no guilt. I had to protect myself at all costs.

. 17 .

Larkin

I walked out the door into the courtyard. The bright light caused a searing pain behind my left eye. I grabbed my sunglasses, put them on, and looked around for Marco. I saw him sitting by a tree on the other side of the courtyard. He looked fabulously chill as he reclined. A bunch of people I didn't know were seated at picnic tables, most of them chatting quietly. Some were reading novels; others were playing card games. Until that day, I had never eaten out there. I honestly had no real idea that anyone did. It was completely different world from the loud, overcrowded cafeteria.

Marco saw me and waved me over. His smile was large and bright, his white teeth shining in the sun. I walked to him with a small spring in my step, breathing in the fresh air, "Hey! I like it out here."

"Yeah, it's pretty cool. I prefer it out here," I said

"I can see why."

"Have a seat."

"Under this beautiful tree? Why yes, I think I will," I curtsied. "In fact, I may sit here all day." I added in a sing-song voice. The lush grass under the tree called to me almost as much as Marco did. I sat and grabbed my apple and cottage cheese from my bag, ready to start fake eating again. He was eating a sandwich, hummus with tortilla chips, and fruit.

"So, Larkin. I know we've just met, but I've really been thinking about our, um, run-in." He looked at me quizzically. "What was going on?"

"You don't want to hear about my problems. Let's talk about something fun."

He dipped a tortilla in the hummus, "Okay then, what would be fun for you to talk about?"

I looked at him and winked. "So, Marco, what's your story?"

"What would you like to know?" I felt his elbow touch mine as we both leaned against the trunk of the tree.

"Why did you move here?"

"What can I say? I'm a world traveler."

"Really?"

He returned my wink. "Sort of. So, um, you gonna eat that apple, or just   hold it the entire time. You'll get pretty hungry if you just hold onto it like an accessory."

"Oh, right, I forgot I had it in my hand." I took a small bite. I had to keep talking, if I kept talking, I wouldn't have time to take a bite. I changed the subject quickly, "So, do you know where you're going next year?"

"Dr. Smith is planning a trip for me to go on a few campus visits, longer ones. You know, the ones where you live with a student and follow them around for a few days while sitting in on classes. You should talk to her about doing that."

"When?"

"End of September."

"Where?"

"Dickinson first, then Stone Valley, and then this small school in Maryland, Chesapeake College? She said it would be perfect for me, but I don't know."

We looked at each other. "Okay, you know what? I'm going to make an appointment to talk to her. I need to get serious about next year." To be honest, I hadn't even started thinking about applying to schools yet. It felt like a huge pressure on my chest. Everything was so up in the air with my health problems. My doctor had suggested a gap year, but it was good to start looking anyway. I mean, it was my senior year.

"So, what about you?" he asked.

"What do you mean?"

"Who is Larkin?" he looked me in the eye.

"Um, I don't know what to say?"

"Okay? We'll start easy. What do you do on the weekends?"

"I don't know. I've been so sick for so long. I sort of lost myself."

"Yeah, I've noticed people talking about that. They seem excited to have you back."

"I have Post-Concussion Syndrome. It's been two years now."

"Two years? Really?"

"Really. That's why I haven't been here and why everyone knows me. I was here before."

"That explains that. What's Post-Concussion Syndrome?" he asked timidly.

"Basically, I had a really bad concussion that didn't heal. I also had a fractured skull."

"Shit. How'd it happen?"

"On the soccer field." I didn't want to go into my more detail than that. I could feel my heart rate rise.

"So, you've had a concussion for two years? Do you still have symptoms?"

"Yeah, some. Mostly some lingering light sensitivity and headaches," I said quietly. "I was basically in bed the whole time." I didn't want to tell him about the PTSD, Anxiety, and supposed Anorexia. Those were embarrassing and, honestly, I felt ashamed.

He took a bite of his lunch, obviously thinking. Obviously feeling awkward, I sat staring at my shoes.

"So, let's just say that I'm in a period of self re-creation," I added in, trying to change the subject.

"Self re-creation is always good," he replied.

"Yeah, I think so! I can change my persona. It's been so long since anyone has really known me, I could be anything."

"The sky's the limit!"

"I'm thinking hippie hobo; they seem pretty peaceful and happy."

"Or movie star . . . oh no! Rock star."

"Heck, yeah! I could have groupies and paparazzi following me."
That's not anxiety inducing at all.

He handed me a Tostito. I didn't want it, but I took it and ate it. I calculated the calories.

"What do YOU do in the summers?" I asked him, returning the favor.

"I go home to Guatemala."

"Really? You're from Guatemala? You don't have an accent or anything."

"I am. Actually, I was adopted when I was a baby, but I've been going back since I was 13 to help out in the orphanage."

"Oh wow! That's really, really great!"

"It's important to me." He looked me in the eye. "Sometimes it's hard to come back though. I just feel like there is so much that needs to be done there."

I saw a deep longing in his eyes. I mean, here was a guy who truly wanted to help people. It was different from what I was used to. Different goals than just spending the whole summer at Brooke's pool, or going to parties.

"Well, I'm glad you came back. You seem to be someone that I can really talk to," I said.

He said nothing after that, just placed his arm down closer to mine. For a moment, our forearms touched.

"The bell's about to ring." I put my hands over my ears. He looked at me and smiled the sweetest smile, then put his arm around my shoulder to cradle me close to him. The ringing was much louder out there. The pain in my head grew a little bit, but it didn't matter, nothing could shake me right then. I felt safe.

We both stood, stretched, and grabbed our bags.

"Creative Writing. You going to be okay?" He was referring to my panic attack and punching Luke.

"I think so. I'll just try to stick near you," I said with a smile. I meant it. There was something different with him. Maybe it was the fact that he was a good guy, or maybe it was because he was the first person I let hold me close? I don't know, but I felt safe.

"I really like the idea of that."

"Alright, let's do this."

We walked out of the peaceful courtyard into the noisy hallway. I didn't shrink down this time; I didn't feel the need to. We stopped at each of our lockers and walked to class together.

. 18 .

Reagan

I walked toward the lunchroom slowly, plotting. I had a million questions firing off in my brain. *What if Larkin was there? What if Luke was sitting next to her? Why did he feel sorry for her? She punched him! I needed to do something to stop this. I needed to convince people that she was not who they thought she was.*

As I walked, I felt as if I was going into battle. I looked around. Everyone was whispering. The rumors were already flying around about how she punched Luke and how he put his arm around her. They knew I was pissed; they were watching to see what I would do next. I had my reputation to protect. I was about to create a bad situation for her, and that made me happy. I was taking control. My determination ramped up as I walked. I held my shoulders higher. I lifted my chin and kept my eyes straight forward.

I reached the double doors to the cafeteria, pushed them open, and scanned the room. I walked to my table with a sense of purpose. I knew what I needed to do: keep the momentum going after physics lab. I threw my bag on the table where everyone was already eating. I didn't see Larkin anywhere and, honestly, I felt let down. I wanted to mess with her. It was okay though; Brooke was there. My eyes locked onto hers. We stared at each other until Sophie grabbed my attention.

"I don't know, it's just strange," Sophie said.

"What's strange?" Brooke asked.

And that was how it started.

"Brooke, I know she's your girl, but think about it. Have you ever heard of someone taking two years to heal from a CONCUSSION?" I stared directly at Brooke as I asked this.

"Reagan, don't. We aren't doctors."

"Right. But Brooke, she literally disappeared. And now she's back like nothing ever happened?"

"I think it's pretty obvious she's not just here as if nothing ever happened," Brooke responded with a snap in her voice.

"I'm just saying, there's something we don't know. It doesn't add up."

"IT'S NOT FOR US TO ADD UP," Brooke said, her loudly.

"Look, don't snap at us. She came back and on her first day and punched Luke in the face." Izzy said loudly, "Then Luke went over to her house? What happened there? Was she always this abusive to him?"

"Oh, good Lord. Give me a break! You've never heard of a panic attack?" Brooke looked shocked, then irate.

"I'm just saying. This is weird."

"Don't mess with her! Don't mess with me!"

Brooke was getting defensive and it was perfect. It was enough to make people doubt Larkin.

"True. I know one thing for sure, she's been taking boxing lessons, so I better not point out the obvious, that she's faking the whole thing," I snapped back. Everyone started laughing. I had won them. "But I will give you one thing. She's so skinny and pathetic looking now. Disgusting. I'm surprised she didn't break her fist when she hit him."

"Oh my God. Don't start this, Reagan," Brooke warned.

I had never seen Brooke look that pissed off before. It was kind of a refreshing change. I have to admit, she was fun to play with.

With a smirk on my face, I turned to get in the lunch line. I didn't realize Luke was in back of me the whole time. He didn't say a word; he had no reaction. His face was blank.

"Hey baby! there you are," I said as I batted my eyelashes.

"Don't, just don't. You don't understand what you are doing," he said, then turned and left.

My stomach dropped to the floor. I never expected him to hear any of that. I needed him to see me as the loving supportive girlfriend. I needed him to see me as sweet and innocent. I followed after him and grabbed his arm.

"Baby, I'm just worried about you. She HIT you and that scares me. I'm mad because she hurt you."

"She was in the middle of a panic attack. I shouldn't have grabbed her. It was my fault. DO NOT turn this into something it's not." He pulled his arm out of my grasp.

"I understand that, but look at it from my perspect . . ."

"STOP, just stop. I know what you are doing. I've seen you do it before. You ruin people, that's what you do. Don't do it to her," Luke said through his teeth. The muscles in his jawline were tense.

I just looked at him, saying nothing.

I grabbed his arm again and put my body in front of his. "Look at me."

"I'm looking," he said with eyes so cold that I got a shiver down my spine.

"I'm worried about losing you. I love you. We've done so much together, but I know you never fully got over her." I started talking non-stop as my eyes teared up. Crying always worked with him, but this time they were legitimate tears. I knew I was about to lose him, and I couldn't hold it in.

He sighed and grabbed a hold of me tightly, hugging me. "Don't get upset. I was just worried about her. That's all," he whispered before he gently kissed me on the head. "Besides, she's out in the courtyard with Marco anyway. You have nothing to be concerned about."

"Marco who?" I asked.

I genuinely had no idea who Marco was, but if Larkin was in the courtyard with another guy, that guy just became my new favorite person. A sense of security rushed over me. All I had to do was make sure that relationship happened. If I did that, I would look like a nice person, a matchmaker, even. Everyone would look at me like I was the hero. My mom would be proud of me. And I would get to keep Luke to myself. It was a win-win.

. 19 .

Larkin

I sat on the couch at Juice and Java sipping my steaming hot Jasmine Green tea while enjoying the solo guitarist playing folk tunes. Around me people enjoyed green smoothies, salads, and iced coffees with whipped cream overflowing. The ambiance was warm and cozy. Some people sat at small tables chatting while others were on their laptops or phones. The person in the armchair next to me was typing away on his laptop. I checked my email on my phone while I waited for Brooke. I went into a daydream state, wondering what my life would have been like had the accident never happened. Would I have ended up horrible like Reagan?

Suddenly Brooke plopped down beside me on the leather couch. "Hey, Lark!"

"Hey! Cozy in here." We gave each other a side hug.

"I'm so happy you're back, I missed you so much."

"Awe, did you? I missed you too."

"I did. I was forced to hang out with Reagan. You just don't even know."

"Okay, yeah. That sounds like a special kind of hell."

"Oh honey, you have no idea." We both laughed.

"What's up with Reagan taking over my life." I rolled my eyes not so subtly.

"Girl, she really did. She started in on Luke about a week after your injury and just wouldn't give up. I think she just wore him down like a virus. With soccer though? She cost us so many games with soft goals during sophomore year. We really needed you. She would become enraged anytime anyone would mention you. It was insane."

"I didn't even keep up with the team once I was hurt. It was just too much to worry about. Sorry."

"I know. Don't worry about that. We understood."

"I missed everyone. I really missed you Brooke," I said as her order came up.

There weren't many people in the world sweeter than Brooke. I started thinking that maybe there was a mix up in communication. Maybe it was all a misunderstanding. That they didn't realize what was happening, they just knew I dropped off the face of the earth. I was trying to find some reason why I shouldn't be upset with her. I wondered if I should be feeling guilty for feeling so mad. They had their own stuff going on, but they seemed to be happy that I was back, so that was something. Right?

They called Brooke's number again, she popped up and went to the counter behind the couch. She came back with her heaping Caesar salad and green machine smoothie. "You aren't getting anything to eat?

"Nah, I had a big lunch," I said, thinking back to my bite of apple, "and my parents are taking us out to dinner." I had become good at lying so I wouldn't be forced to eat.

"Cool!" she looked me up and down. "You really have slimmed down."

"Thanks! I just try to eat healthy," I answered. I felt like my hard work was paying off. Brooke had no idea. Hell, I had no idea. But yes, my body was completely different from the muscular athlete I was in the past.

"It's hard . . . you know I want that grilled cheese and muffin. You KNOW I do."

"Ha! So do I. I'm actually starting to salivate," I said, even though the thought of a grilled cheese and a muffin sounded positively revolting to me. *How do they even go together?*

I quietly sipped my tea while she devoured her salad. Something about the sound people made when eating crispy things made me angry, but with the guitar music going, I couldn't hear it too badly. Honestly though, food in general angered me.

"Brooke, can I ask you a question?"

"Of course."

"Why didn't you visit me after I got home from the hospital?"

"Oh Lark, your mom said the doctor wanted you to do nothing but rest, that you'd be able to call when you were ready." Brooke looked visibly upset, "I mean, the longer it took to hear from you, the more I worried. But my mom said that sleep was what you needed. Everyone said you couldn't have any stimulation. And, well, the months just dragged on and on, and we thought maybe that it was too late. It's a stupid thought, but we didn't understand what was going on."

"Okay. After a while though, why didn't you call?"

"I guess the school year started, and we made States. You know how little time you have when that happens. I was never home. I missed you though, so much. Please know that I missed you."

"It was lonely lying in bed all the time. I felt like my world was closing in on me." I started to worry that I was saying too much, but I kept going, "I felt like I was going insane. I had doctors' appointments and stuff, but it would take days to recuperate from those." I started to tear up. "I just, It was just really hard."

"Larkin, I should have beaten down your front door. I didn't know it was like that. I'm so sorry." She put her salad down on the coffee table and slid her arm around me. I saw tears in her eyes. "I feel awful about it."

"I know, I'm sorry. I didn't mean to make you feel that way. I just needed to talk about it."

"No, we need to talk about it." Brooke's face suddenly changed; it looked harder, mad. "I just, I need to tell you something, but I don't want you to get upset."

"Okay?" I felt like the floor was going to fall from under me. "Reagan is starting some sort of campaign against you." She looked me in the eyes and grabbed my hand before continuing, "I got into an argument with her in the cafeteria about it. She's trying to make people believe you're faking all this."

"Faking being stuck in bed for two years? Why would anyone choose that?" I felt my heart rate start to rise. My face was getting hot and I began to shake. "She was there when I got kicked in the head. She was there with the team in the hospital."

"I know. Larkin, listen. This isn't even about you; this is about her and Luke. I'm sure of it."

"Is everyone believing her?" I felt my eyes well up. I was never looking for sympathy, but I never imagined people wouldn't believe me.

"Honestly, I don't know. But they won't if I have anything to say about it," she said and she squeezed my hand harder. "I got your back." She quickly changed the subject. "You've been hanging out with Marco lately. What's that about?" She gave me a side eye and a smile.

A man in hiking gear came into the café at that point. The Appalachian Trail runs through our area, so we would see hikers. He was in need of a shower, obviously, because the scent of patchouli overtook the entire place. He threw his backpack next to the couch we were sitting on, then walked to the counter. We ignored it.

"Marco? I literally ran into him yesterday. Made his papers fly everywhere. It was a freaken mess." We both started laughing and I wiped a single tear away from my cheek. "I was a complete spaz. I can't even . . ."

She laughed, "Really?"

"Oh yeah, we both fell over. Totally put a rip in my favorite leggings. I probably almost killed him."

"And now you're best friends? Girl!!!"

"Oh no, he kept trying to catch up to me to see how I was, so I agreed to eat lunch with him."

"I saw that! I wonder why I never ate lunch out there. Seems better than the cafeteria." She elbowed me in my arm. "But I have to be honest, it looked like you were getting a little cozy under that tree," she blurted out, raising an eyebrow. "I mean, it's not like I was spying or anything. But I'm sure someone else was."

"Luke?"

"Oh, I'm sure. He walked into the cafeteria looking like he was about to kill someone. Then he overheard Reagan talking about you. I can tell he wasn't happy . . . at all."

"Well, crap. No, you know what? Good, I hope he saw us," I said with a nod. I had to admit, I did wish he was still mine, but he wasn't. I wanted to stay as far away from Reagan's shitstorm as I could.

Brooke started speaking in a breathy tone, "Dahhhling, he looked positively nettled." We laughed again.

Thank God we had that moment. I felt a little bit of peace laughing with her. "What about you? Are you dating anyone?"

"I have my eyes on someone, but he's completely unattainable and should probably stay that way. So, I just stare at him from afar," Brooke said as she breathed sigh.

"Who?"

"Okay, okay." She took a sip of her Green Machine Smoothie. In a small voice that was almost impossible to hear, she squeaked, "Vincent."

"What? Wait. What?" Vincent was known for one thing, and it was not a good thing. "I mean, I get it, he is hot as all get out, but you are so-"

"What, Larkin, what am I?"

"NICE!"

"I know. I think that's part of it. I'm always nice. Maybe I just want to live life on the edge once in a while."

"You know what? I get that. I really do. So, what do we have to do to get him to ask you to homecoming?"

"Oh gosh, I'm sure he wouldn't even go to homecoming." We both nodded. "Well, let's work on a way to get him there with you."

She looked at me for a little while. "Okay, let's just concentrate on you and Marco. My dad would freak if I got with Vincent, anyway."

"Stop it with Marco already! We were just chatting."

"Mmm hmmm, right. Look, I get it, the heart wants what the heart wants." I fake punched her arm. We talked for a little while longer and I found out that she was applying to Penn State and Pitt. Both were schools that had been scouting her for about a year. We also talked about the pool party, which sounded like it would be huge. I told her I would go, but I didn't want anyone to see me in a bikini. I watched her eat some more as I sipped my tea.

The feeling of hunger was completely gone by then. Once you hit a certain point, your body just expects to not get food. I thought that maybe if I could get my run in that evening, I could eat something small before bed.

As we got up to leave, the hiker slid onto the couch we had been using. He looked thankful to have someplace comfortable to sit.

While I was lying in bed that night, I worried about what Reagan was telling people. I couldn't stop thinking about it. It enraged me. I had to say something to her. I knew I shouldn't, but I had to.

. 20 .

Larkin: My health issues are off limits to you.
Reagan: What are you talking about, crazy person?
Larkin: Reagan, shut the hell up. Would you do this to a cancer patient?
Reagan: Oh honey, now you're trying to compare yourself to a cancer patient? You really are a mess, aren't you?
Larkin: You have no idea what I've been through.
Reagan: Oh wah-wah, and that means that you can now steal my boy friend?
Larkin: WTH are you talking about?
Reagan: I know you want him back. Stay the hell away.
Larkin: Are you serious right now? You know, I pity you. You must be a wreck inside.
Reagan: Whatever, bitch. Don't come for me, and I won't come for you. Got it?
Larkin: Get over yourself.
Reagan: Oh, I think you should take that advice for yourself. You should stay home from the pool party.
Larkin: It's at my best friend's house. I'll be there.
Reagan: So sad for you that your best friend ignored you for two years. Desperate much?

***

Marco: Hey, Phil. I just wanted to say hi!
Larkin: That's sweet! Hi!
Marco: Wanna meet up tomorrow?
Larkin: I have to go to Brooke's pool party. Wanna come?
Marco: No thanks, the jocks aren't my crowd. You sure you don't just want to catch a movie or something?
Larkin: Sorry, I can't. Maybe next weekend?
Marco: Sounds good.

Larkin:	Thank you for hanging out with me at lunch.
Marco:	I hope we can do it again.
Larkin:	We will!

***

Coach:	Larkin, I heard you were back to school. Listen, I talked to your mom about this already. Would you like to be a student coach for my 8 year-old girls' team? I need a goalie trainer. It would be good for you to get on the pitch again.
Larkin:	Oh, my mom didn't say anything. What would I have to do?
Coach:	Just check with your doctor and get cleared for it. I'll email you the form.
Larkin:	Okay. Thanks.
Coach:	I'm excited to have you back. This will be a good experience for you.

. 21 .

Larkin

I woke up, jolting up out of my bed as if gasping for air, my night-clothes wet from sweat. It took me a while to realize that I was safe.

The visions of falling, the ball, and the girl coming at me were still raw in my mind. I took a deep breath, trying to clear my head. I could smell the bacon wafting in through my bedroom door.

It was Saturday, so I laid back down thinking about the pool party. If I went downstairs my mom would make me eat, and eating was the one thing I absolutely did not want to do. I needed to be in a swimsuit that afternoon. I knew the only way I would get out of breakfast was by sleeping late. My mother would never wake me up. "She needs her sleep," repeated over and over had an effect on my mother. So, I closed my eyes and thought about the week.

I felt my body start to relax and slowly drift back to sleep.

The dreams started again, the crowd cheering, then gasping, blackness, and then I couldn't hear. Nothingness. Spiraling dark nothingness.

Suddenly a small body flopped on my bed next to me. My youngest brother breathed into my face.

"Get up, get up, get up."

"I'm up, I'm up! Stop!"

"Mommy has breakfast ready. Come eat."

"I'll be down in a minute," I said lazily as I sat up. He grabbed me in a hug and then ran out of the room yelling to mom that I was coming.

I slowly placed my feet on the hardwood floor of my room, contemplating how to get out of eating. I had options. I could carry a little bag with me to put the food in. I could eat two bites and push everything around on the plate until my mom just went away. The thought of making myself throw up came into my mind again, but I knew that was crossing a line I wasn't prepared for.

I walked down the steps, hands lightly holding the bannister, thinking. I planned to talk a lot, which was a tactic I used often. It worked for me.

"Morning mom," I said as I wrapped my arms around her.

"Morning, Lark. Your breakfast is at your spot. I have to get your brother to soccer, so please make sure to eat. DO NOT throw it away."

"Mommy, I won't. I'll eat." I smiled at her innocently.

"Good. Go, sit," she ordered. "Oh, I made an appointment to get your coaching forms signed. It's Wednesday at 4:00."

"Okay. Do you really think I'm ready?"

"Judging by how much you run, I think you can handle a bunch of little kids. I know you miss soccer, so I think it will be good for you."

"Yea, probably," I nodded. "Where are the boy's games today?"

"One in Carlisle and one in Palmyra. Only an hour apart if I drive fast, so it will be a miracle if we get to Palmyra in time," Mom said, frantically trying to find the top to my brother's water bottle.

"Soccer mom or speed demon?" I asked, acting like I was doing a voice over for a movie trailer.

She pointed to the kitchen table. "Stop talking and go eat," she said.

"FINE!" I rolled my eyes and turned to follow her command. As I approached the table, I shielded the look of disgust on my face. Why did she insist on making these big breakfasts? She used to just give us cereal or a pop tart and go on with her day. Once she noticed I was losing weight, the breakfasts became truly gluttonous. The amount of food I had to throw away was absurd.

"What are you up today?" she asked.

"Brooke is having a pool party."

My mom turned around excitedly . . . too excitedly.

"Oh, honey, I'm so glad you are going out and doing things! I was worried your anxiety would stop you."

"Mom, stop."

She was crying. Of course, she was crying. "I'm just so proud of you."

"Oookay?" I tried not to roll my eyes. I understood. She'd been so worried about me for so long, seeing me do something besides lying in bed was a big deal. But I can tell you, I was not as excited as she was. People would be drinking and eating . . . in their swimsuits! I had been in bed for two years. I didn't want to be in a bikini around those people.

I sat down to stare at my plate as my mom and brothers rushed out the door. As soon as they left, I got up and shoved my food into the garbage disposal. After my plate was clean, I grabbed a handful of grapes and a mug of black coffee. A much better option for me, for sure. I didn't want anything that would make my stomach look larger.

I ran up my steps with the goal of finding a bathing suit that covered me enough to hide my body. As I passed the bathroom, I spotted my scale. It called to me. Everyone warned me not to weigh myself too much, not to become obsessed, but I had to. I needed to get below 90 pounds. I couldn't let anyone know that was my goal, but it was. I even did the coin trick, carrying coins in my pockets during weigh-ins at my doctor's appointments. But I felt like it was necessary. They couldn't know how close to 90 I really was. I'd end up in the hospital again. But that didn't matter. No one understood my obsession over this goal.

I slid out of my clothes and looked in the mirror. Absolutely disgusting. My stomach pooched out. My thighs touched at the top. My arms were entirely too big. My face was incredibly round. Nothing about me was right.

After taking a deep breath, I slowly stepped on the scale. 92 pounds. I felt like I was going to faint. I had gained a pound. My heart started beating faster. I was finding it hard to breathe. I was sweating. I immediately grabbed my pjs, went to my room and put on my workout clothes. I ran down the steps and out the front door. *I will do at least five miles today!* I vowed to myself.

. 22 .

Reagan

"Iz, what do you think of this one? Should I buy it?" I held up the bikini in my hand.

"It's white. If you get wet everyone will be able to see through it," she said, nodding.

"Isn't that the point? Besides, my tan will look darker in white"

"Ummm, no. Look, here's a cute pink one."

"Cute is NOT going to get Luke to notice me."

"Okay. Red, you'll look hot."

"True."

"I'm going with this brown one," Izzy said, grabbing a light brown string bikini off the rack and holding it in the air. "I'm loving the bead embellishments."

"THAT will look perfect on you!" I found a red string bikini in my size. "Here it is! This one is mine."

We turned toward the changing rooms, happy about our finds.

"Okay, so how are you going to get Luke's attention again. I mean, you don't think you're close to breaking up? Do you?" Izzy asked.

"I don't know, but it can't happen. I need to pull out all the stops."

"Maybe we should tan after this?" Izzy suggested.

"YES! Let's! Just a light glow."

"Exactly," she nodded at me.

We entered dressing rooms next to each other. The light was horrific, showing off every single one of my imperfections. I took off my clothes slowly, but I put the suit on quickly. I stopped and looked at everything that was wrong with my body, all the things my mother would point out. I always hated getting changed in front of mirrors. I hated the way I looked. I never projected it to anyone, but on the inside I spent so much time worrying about how I looked, how I acted, and what I said.

My hair was a mess.

My skin was breaking out because I was eating too much crap. I looked like I was getting fat.

How did I have cellulite at the age of 17? I had dark circles; I needed to sleep more. I needed to work out more; I was flabby.

I didn't want to stand in front of everyone in a bikini. I was sure Luke would break up with me if he saw me like this. No one would stay friends with me. Truthfully, I wasn't that great of a goalie. If Larkin hadn't gotten injured, I wouldn't have my spot and I wouldn't have Luke. I had been lucky, and I knew it. I had nothing to offer anyone.

My legs felt weak. I leaned against the glass of the mirror behind me and slowly sank to the floor. I grabbed my knees and drew them to my chest. Sitting like that always made me feel better; safe even. I sat rocking myself. I was doing anything I could to make the negative thoughts stop.

I looked up at the mirror and looked at myself again.

I slowly found my composure and got back up. Somehow, I found the strength I needed to swing the door open. Izzy was already out there, in her suit, ready to compare.

"Girl, you look HOT!" I said immediately when I saw her, trying to hide the fact that I was upset. And she did look hot!

"You do too! These are perfect," she replied.

"They are! Wait, turn! Bootie check."

"Yep, our booties are poppin."

"Slay?" I asked.

"Slay!" she agreed. "Luke's going to be all over you."

"Hell yeah!" I nodded. "We need to find someone for you!"

"Nah, I'm good. They aren't worth it." Izzy responded. "I just like making them melt."

"Truth."

"Larkin will look ridiculous next to you," she said.

I nodded at her response, but only hoped she was right.

. 23 .

Larkin

My shoes hit the pavement with a rhythmic thud. My legs burned and my lungs felt heavy. My breathing became hard and labored. Sweat soaked my shirt. I kept going; I had to. Pushing myself was the one thing I was always good at. I became hyper-focused, knowing what needed to be done. Luke's house was around the block. I should have turned and gone the other way, but I didn't stop running in the direction of his house. Even though I needed to stay away from him, I was not going to change my path.

I started to feel dizzy but kept running anyway, sure that people would think less of me if I stopped. I was always worried about that. I didn't want someone looking at me thinking I was weak. I thought if I stopped and walked back and forth while taking my pulse, maybe that would look better than just walking home. Like I was walking to check my heartrate, and not because I wasn't able to keep going. So, I stopped and did exactly that. My pulse was almost too fast to count. I knew that wasn't okay. I chose to ignore it.

I walked around the corner and saw Luke washing his Jeep. I was simultaneously excited to see him and scared. I didn't know what to do, go home or say "Hi." I decided to turn and walk the other way. That's when he saw me. There was no going back. I willed myself to catch my breath, to make my heart slow down.

I started jogging again to make it look like I wasn't having trouble. I decided the best thing to do was to just run up and talk to him.

"Hey, Luke!"

"Hey, girl! Are you here to punch me in the nose, or . . ."

"I'm sorry, what was that?" I said with a raised eyebrow.

"Oh nothing, just commenting on what a beautiful young, uh, piece of work you are," he said looking me up and down.

"You must really want a nose job, because if you're a jerk, I'll punch you again." I cracked my knuckles. He acted like he was going to run back into his house. We both started laughing. He came up to me, with his wet shirt, and took a long look assessing me.

"Is that so? 'Punch the Jerk' huh?"

"Oh yeah, bring it JERK!" I danced around as if I was Laila Ali.

"Then you better get ready for this." he moved closer with something behind his back. Hugging me with his wet shirt soaking mine, he proceeded to dump a bucket of soapy water over my head. I squealed and chased after him. I had no idea what my endgame was. If I caught him, what could I possibly do?

He ran around to the back of his house. I spotted another bucket and picked it up. I chased after him with water sloshing all over me, making me even more drenched, if that was even possible. I finally gained ground on him as he turned with his arms up in the air, signaling surrender.

"Oh no, there is no peace accord here. You're getting it."

"Please, please, I beg of you." He dropped to his knees. "Mercy, mercy."

"There's no mercy either." I threw the water in his face. He pounced up quickly and tackled me with his hands behind my head.

Suddenly he was on top of me. Pellets of soapy water dripped from the tip of his nose and hit me in the face.

"I've missed you," he said. I could feel his sweet breath on me. His brown eyes searched inside of mine. He slid his fingers through my wet hair, then brought his warm lips to mine, touching them lightly. His soapy, sweaty scent overtook me. I leaned up into his kiss. I felt weak, and my heart was beating even faster. He gave me a small, sweet peck before sliding off me and sitting up.

"Larkin, I can't tell you how much I've missed you."

"Luke . . ."

"No, please just listen," he pleaded.

"Luke, no, you have a girlfriend. We can't do this. Yes, we were awesome together. Yes, I loved you. But it's been two years."

"I don't love her," he admitted, then stopped talking and looked at me. "You said loved, not love. You don't love me anymore?"

"We can't talk about this while you are with her."

We both got up and looked into each other's eyes. Then he came closer to me and gave me a hug, a big wet hug.

"I'm sorry," he whispered in my ear.

I had shivers . . . butterflies . . . jitters. I was so confused about my feelings. I had started off the week mad at everyone, but moment by moment, the anger was slipping away. I feared losing the anger would leave me open and exposed.

"Maybe someday, but not today," I whispered in response.

I realized I needed to leave. I couldn't stay there after being that close to him. I got up, straightened my clothes, and said, "I need to go. We can talk later." I didn't want to sound like there was anything wrong.

"Come one, babe, please stay and hang out?"

"I can't. We'll talk later. Okay?"

"Promise?" he asked.

"Yes," and I turned and walked home.

I wasn't even in the house when I got the text I was expecting. It was too powerful of a moment for him not to text me right away.

***

Luke: Hey, girl, you dry yet?

Larkin: Barely, actually no. Still dripping.

Luke: Sorry, not sorry. I had too much fun.

Larkin: Well, that's just RUDE! :P

Luke: Oh, you know you had fun too!

Larkin: Luke, we always have fun.

Luke: We do! I've missed you. We have to make up for lost time.

Larkin: We shouldn't make up for lost time.

Waiting, waiting, waiting.

Luke: I can't do anything about the past. I screwed up. I should have never let you go.

Larkin: mmm hmm

Luke: Should I break up with Reagan?

Larkin: You shouldn't have to ask me.

Luke: I'm not breaking up with her if I don't have a chance with you.

Larkin: That's just stupid. The great Luke Stewart is afraid of being alone? Please. This is your decision, and yours only. It has nothing to do with me.

Larkin: I understand loud and clear. Okay, I have to go. Dream of me, babe.

Larkin: rrriiiigggghhhttt.

***

I admitted to myself that the small kiss was pretty amazing, but I wasn't sure if I should go down that road again. Of course, I still had feelings for him. Of course, he made me feel weak in the knees. But, ultimately, this decision was mine. What if I got a secondary concussion? I needed to be sure that he would be with me for that. How often could he possibly deal with panic attacks? How many was too many? How long before he gave up on me? I would rather be alone than grow to rely on someone who was just going to abandon me in the end.

I grabbed some water and flopped down on my couch. I was still wet; still a little out of breath; still a little dizzy. I picked up my phone to check messenger.

***

Marco: Hey!
Larkin: Heyyy, Marco! What's up?

I started feeling really guilty.

Marco: Nothing. Have you decided to skip the party yet?
Larkin: lol. No, sorry, I need to go.
Marco: You feeling up to it?
Larkin: I'll be fine. I probably won't stay too long. I'm not feeling 100%
Marco: Wanna go for an hour then leave to chill with me? I really want to hang out with you.
Larkin: Maybe. Let me see how I feel? I'm actually feeling a little dizzy.

. 24 .

Reagan

I jumped out of Izzy's car and turned around.

"Thanks, Iz, I needed this girl time," I shouted to her through her open door. "I'll see you at the party!"

I dashed up to my front door and threw it open. My mom was in the sunroom doing yoga. I silently closed the door and tried to tip-toe up the steps, not wanting her to ask to see my new bikini. She'd say something bad about it and how I looked in it. I just wanted to enjoy the party; I didn't need her negative thoughts running through my head. I got halfway up the steps and heard her calling me.

"Reagan! What are you up to?"

"Oh nothing. Just got back from hanging with Izzy," I replied without turning around.

"Did you go shopping? What did you get?"

"Just a bathing suit for Brooke's pool party."

"Oh great! Bikini, I hope?"

"Mom, yes, a bikini."

"Go put it on, I want to see it on you," she said with a smile.

"Mom, I just wanna get a shower and get ready for the party."

"Go!" she said sternly. "That way, if you made a bad purchase, we can get it exchanged quickly."

"Fine." I turned and finished climbing the stairs.

I closed my door behind me and leaned against it for a few moments. I had to prepare myself to stand in front of my mother in a bikini. She had this horrible ability to spot every little thing. When I was ready, I took the bikini out of the bag and laid it out on my bed. I began to get undressed. As I put the bikini on, I worried I wouldn't look good enough for her. I took one last look at myself in the swimsuit and opened my bedroom door. It was no surprise that she was already standing there, waiting. She stood with her hands crossed in front of her, her eyes looking me up and down.

"Red? With your skin tone?" she asked.

"I thought it was cute," I replied.

"It is cute, but is it sexy?"

"Really, mom? You want your daughter to look sexy?"

"You should run more. I'm seeing cellulite on your thighs."

"I will," I said. My shoulders slumped over, getting ready for whatever she'd say next.

"Good." She continued to look me over. "Okay. It's good. I approve."

What? She liked it?

"It will get his attention, that's for sure." She nodded. "I'll get you a sexy little wrap to wear over it." She turned to walk to her room, leaving me behind, shocked. She usually hated everything I wore.

"Umm, thanks?"

That's when she turned around, "Right, just make sure to wear some cover up under your eyes. You have dreadful black circles. You might also want to put something on those pimples. You aren't eating chocolate again, are you?" She started talking faster. "Also, do something about your nails. Short nails aren't in and it looks like you've been biting them. You don't want to look like you bite them, that would show you are stressed. Maybe you should go get some press on nails or something," she kept going, faster and faster. "Stressed people don't have it all together."

I followed her into her bedroom. She began going through her drawers looking for the cover-up. "Oh, do make sure to wear the cover-up; it will hide the cellulite. If you have to take it off to get in the pool, do so quickly so Luke doesn't notice." She just wouldn't stop, "Or anyone else for that matter, Good Lord, they'll be calling you thunder thighs in no time." She found the cover-up and turned to hand it to me. I always wondered how my mother could say all those horrible things to me and still keep a smile on her face. But there it was, that smile with those perfectly blinding white teeth.

"Thanks, mom." I simply turned and walked to my room. *Who was I kidding? I would never be enough for her.*

. 25 .

Larkin

I walked around Brook's house to her pool. It had been so long since I had been there. I needed to force myself to walk through the gate. I went in quietly, trying to not let anyone notice me. I thought I looked horrible in my bikini. So horrible that I wasn't planning on taking off my cover up. I wished I could just fade into the background. The music was thumping, surrounding me, piercing my ear drums, making my headache rise. The smell of hot dogs and burgers hung in the air. My stomach started aching. I wanted to throw up. It was way too crowded.

Brooke came running up to me, slamming herself into me for a hug.

"Lark, I'm so glad you're here! Just like the old times. Come on!"

I followed, looking around as I walked behind her. It felt like everyone from the varsity soccer teams were there. *Was I the only one there not on a team?* Everyone else was completely toned and perfect from a summer of conditioning and running. I felt like I was nothing but flab.

"Lark! Put your stuff down and get in!" Isabel yelled to me, waving her arms frantically. Her well-toned, tanned arms. Ugh.

"I will!" Instead I put my stuff on a recliner and sat.

"You comin' in?" Brooke asked.

I felt eyes on me. They were staring at me. Why were they staring at me?

"I will. You go ahead." Dance music was playing loudly in the background. The thumping was pounding in my ears. Everyone looked like they belonged here, like it was so natural for them. They had all become closer while I was gone. I was an outsider. I looked around. Luke was in the hot tub with Reagan. I tried not to stare. Suddenly the sounds, the smell, everything was putting so much pressure on me. I felt like I was being crushed and my heart felt like it was spasming. Brian did a cannonball. Cold water hit my face like a wave. When he came up, he was laughing; it was piercing.

"Sorry, Larkin. But since you're wet, you might as well get in! Nothing holding you back now," he yelled to me. I just smiled. Tightly.
I thought that if I just left then no one would have cared. But I couldn't. I was stuck there in my recliner.

I leaned back hoping they'd think I was happy and would leave me alone.

"Larkin, come on!" Brooke was standing next to me, dripping on me, smiling at me from under her oversized sunglasses. "Try out the new slide! Let's do this!"

I couldn't say no. What would she think of me if I said no? "Okay," I said, but I stopped in my tracks.

I worried if I got up everyone would see me in my swimsuit. I started shaking. But I had to do this. It was now or never.

I pulled off my bathing suit cover and quickly followed behind Brooke, holding my arms over me, trying to hide myself as best as I could. I tried to make my body as small as possible, hunching over so no one would notice me. Brooke got to the stone steps of the slide and turned around. Her eyes looked me up and down. She was scanning my body.

I felt like I was dying inside.

I knew what everyone else saw. I knew they thought I was too skinny, but that wasn't my truth.

"Lark, are you okay?" she saw the tears well up in my eyes. She came closer to me and lowered her voice. "Is there something else going on? Something other than the head injury?"

I shook my head no, "I'm fine. I just haven't had the conditioning everyone else here had this summer."

"Okay. Well, I'm here for you. I want to make up for not bursting into your room when you were injured." She grabbed my hand and pulled me up the steps. Once at the top we stood side by side. "It's really pretty up here isn't it?" she asked. I nodded in agreement. They had added a lot since I had been there before. It was a natural looking pool, built with rocks with plants surrounding it. It was made to look like a lake, only cleaner.

"You go first. I'll follow," she said to me. I would have done anything to stop from having to stand at the top of that rock mound any longer. It was like I was on a stage and all the world was looking.

I slid down and splashed into the cold saltwater. The momentum of the slide carried me to the deep end of the pool. While under water, I looked for ways to sit on the bottom and never come up. Not necessarily to drown, just to disappear. But my body defied me and carried me to the top. I broke through the surface and gasped. I felt splashing from behind as Brooke shot out from the slide and into the pool and came up laughing.

I was shaking while treading water, not because the water was cold, but because I really didn't want to come back up. I swam to the side of the pool to get out. Brooke followed me.

"I know, I'm shivering too, I wish my parents would have sprung for a heated pool," she said as we walked. She had no idea that I was shaking because, for the first time, I had contemplated death. "Let's get a burger. You look like you could use it."

Everyone was always trying to feed me burgers. What was it about burgers, I mean, seriously?

"I'm not hungry, but I'll come with you."

She rolled her eyes at me, grabbed my hand, and led me to the grill. She got two burgers, plopped them on buns, loaded them up with lettuce mayo and ketchup, and then grabbed an entire bag of chips.

"Grab two cokes," she instructed.

I quickly calculated the caloric value of everything she picked up. The amount of food she had was way over the caloric value of what I allowed myself for a week.

"Let's go sit at that table."

We sat and I started the charade of eating. It was harder with a burger because I couldn't move it around my plate.

"Is Vincent coming?" I asked her.

"No way. My dad would freak if he saw him here. He is not a fan."

"I can understand that. But there is something about a bad guy. Super-hot!" I replied.

She shoved a huge bite of burger in her mouth along with a couple of fries. I could see the half-eaten food in her mouth while she talked. I tried not to cringe.

"Yeah, there's just something sexy about sneaking around, but it's not happening. I can't get his attention." She swallowed her mouth full of food.

"You should just boldly ask him out."

"I wish," she sighed. "I just wish my dad could see what I see in him." She took another bite, then kept talking. "He's a really sweet guy. He just looks . . . rough."

"He does, but if you like him why not try?"

"Yeah, there are too many eyes. My dad knows everyone, and everyone reports back."

"Just be careful."

"I will. Don't worry about me." She stopped talking and looked at me thoughtfully. "Lark, I'm worried about you."

"Why? I'm doing so much better."

"You are so skinny. I couldn't tell until now," she said, looking at me.

I started tuning her voice out. I already knew the drill of that talk and I didn't need to listen to it again. It was the same thing everyone always said. What all the doctors said. What the therapist said. It was all the same. They told my mom it was a control thing because I had no control over my life while I was stuck in bed. They didn't see what I saw. Two years of no cardio, no training, no lifting, and no running. When someone lays in bed and does nothing one thing happens, weight gain, and it happens fast. No one ever understood this. No one. No one had been stuck in bed the way I was. How could they have possibly understood?

"I'm fine. I just lost some muscle mass because I was stuck in bed," I tried to assure her.

"You're eating?" she asked, eyeing my uneaten burger.

"Of course! I'm just not eating right now because I'd rather talk to you."

"Okay, I'm going to go play hostess and let you eat. I'll be back," she said, then got up and left to greet some new arrivals.

I looked at the burger, broke it apart with my hands to make it look like I had eaten some, then walked over to the trash can to throw it away. I went to the cooler and grabbed a water. I planned on walking back to my chair, but I heard my name.

I turned around to see who called me. And I couldn't breathe, it was Reagan, she was sitting on Luke's lap in the hot tub. I tried to get out of my mind that just a few hours before, he was kissing me.

"Hey, Larkin. Looking good in your bikini." She laughed as she stroked the back of Luke's head. "Looks like you are on that starvation diet."

I didn't say anything back. I turned to walk away.

She yelled after me, "Yeah, walk away, little girl."

I heard Luke say something to her, but I couldn't make out what it was.

"Baby, it's okay, I was nice," she said to him in an innocent voice, then laughed again.

My muscles tensed up. I was seeing red. Everything started swirling in my mind. I had to say something, and I had to say it right then and there.

"You know what, Reagan? Shut the hell up! You have no idea what you are talking about."

I became even more enraged when she laughed again, wrapped her arms around Luke's neck, and said, "See baby? I told you she was insane."

"Reagan, stop!" Luke snapped. He looked angry. "Get off me. I need a drink."

Reagan stood up slowly, giving me a long dirty look. It sent shivers down my spine.

"Whatever," I heard her say once she was up.

Luke got out of the hot tub and looked at me.

"I'm sorry," he said as he turned and walked to the cooler.

Reagan got out of the hot tub after him. She walked in my direction. I didn't know what was about to happen, but I tensed in anticipation. My chest started to hurt from holding my breath.

"Bitch," she said with her upper lip sneering as she walked past me, making sure her shoulder knocked into mine.

I lost my balance a little bit, but I didn't fall. I stood my ground.

As she walked away, I could hear her fake whine, "Ouch, Larkin! Your shoulder is so boney. It cut me."

I needed to get out of there. My heart started to feel as if it was going to beat out of my chest. To make matters worse, everyone was staring at me.

My mind was racing, telling me:
I shouldn't have come here. I should have stayed home. They all hate me.
That's why they didn't visit me. They were happy I was gone.
I'm nothing.
I was never anything.

I grabbed my ears. The vibrations of the music felt like an ice pick in my head. Everything was going black. I thought that was it, that I was dying. I turned as quickly as I could. Stumbling. My feet were getting tangled with each other. The world was spinning. Tripping, I ran out the gate into Brooke's front yard.

Somehow, I manage to get to my car. I turned the key to start the engine, blasted the air conditioner, and pointed all the vents directly at my face. I began to breathe deeply, listening to the hum of my car and the air conditioner. I sat for a while with my eyes closed, trying to get my brain to calm itself. Breathing in my mouth, out my mouth, over and over again.

I started to calm down, then it hit me.

I had seen Reagan and Luke kiss. They were kissing right in front of me. He was kissing her the way he used to kiss me, the way he had just kissed me that afternoon. That was when I started questioning myself. Did I want him back? Why was it bothering me that they were kissing; they were together; they were a couple. Of course, they were kissing. Did I still love him?

An overwhelming sadness overtook the panic. Tears ran down my cheeks, and onto my lap. I started having dark thoughts. Thoughts that told me I had lost everything and that my life truly did end the moment I was injured. What was the point of anything anymore?

I laid my head on my steering wheel and began to weep.

. 26 .

Reagan

As I watched her leave, I couldn't help but laugh. She was practically running away from the pool party. I could see her shoulders heaving from where I was. I honestly couldn't believe it.

"What was THAT about?" Izzy asked as she swooped in next to me.

"Just part of the plan," I replied.

She laughed, "Well, that was quick."

We stood next to each other watching as Larkin sat in her Scion. She was obviously crying or hyperventilating or something.

"Did you notice how skinny she is now? It's sickening. I'd feel bad for her if she weren't Larkin," I said to Izzy.

"I hear you. But hey, Luke's all over you!"

"Yeah, well, I have to deal with him now."

"What do you mean?"

"He's so protective over her. I made her look like the whiny bitch she is, and now he's mad at me."

The end of summer sun was blaring and scorching. Everyone was back in the pool after eating. The noise was loud as they all splashed and yelled for each other.

Someone screamed, "Cannonball!" We got hit with a large spray of water.

"Shit," Izzy said, looking down at her now soaked body. She turned to me and asked, "Why is he protective of her? How in the world could he be mad at you?"

"Oh, you know, I may have said some things to her that he thought was harsh. Whatever."

"Ahhh, not surprised by that. You were just trying to keep what is rightfully yours."

"It's okay. His memory will snap back to me." I turned to go to Luke. As I did, I looked over my shoulder at Izzy and said, "I didn't buy this red bikini for nothing. I'm in control. I know what I need to do."

"You got this, girl!" Izzy called after me. "And have fun making up." I turned to see her sly smile.

"You know I will. I just have to turn on the tears." I said with a pout and a fake frown plastered across my face. I turned around to find Luke and make my appeal.

I walked around the pool to where Luke was having a conversation and laughing with his friends. I could tell he was bragging about something. Everyone was hanging on his every word, as always. He saw me but ignored me, acting as if he hadn't noticed me walking toward him. I realized he was actually really pissed at me this time; it showed in his eyes when he looked at me for that brief instant. It was such a fast look that I'm sure no one else noticed, but I had been with him long enough to know the look. Hard. Cold. Steel. It was a look that caused shivers to go down my spine, and not the good kind. It was the type of look that makes someone feel cold in their soul. That should have been a warning to me. It wasn't.

"Reagan! Come here," Jess yelled at me, laughing. I took a quick glance in her direction but did not respond.

Luke changed his course to talk to Aaron who was standing to the left of him, which meant he turned his back toward me. He didn't even want to look at me.

I immediately went into a conversation in my mind.

Oh, What the hell?

Figure out what to say.

How do I fix this?

He's really pissed.

Why is he so pissed?

He loves her.

He wants her back! Fix this!

FIX THIS!

After what seemed like an eternity, I finally approached him. His friends were all laughing around me. They didn't even notice I was standing there. I tapped him on the shoulder. He knew it was me, but he didn't turn. He was ignoring me.

"Luke," I said in a sheepish voice, placing my hand on his shoulder and holding it there. He turned his head to look at me from his peripheral vision, then shook his shoulder trying to get my hand off him. The guys around us noticed and became quiet and wide eyed. A few of them smirked as if they were excited by the unfolding drama.

"Luke, please?" I pleaded.

"You don't want to do this here or now. Trust me," he said with a gruff voice, facing ahead, not looking at me.

"Luke. Baby," I begged again, not touching him anymore.

He turned quickly toward me; I could feel the anger in his eyes. He grabbed my arm and pulled me along the pathway beside the pool. Everyone stopped what they were doing. I heard the splashing stop. The talking ceased. Silence. They were all staring at me. They were all staring at him as he pulled me behind him. His grip was tight on my arm. It hurt.

All I kept thinking was:

This isn't happening.

I can't believe this is happening.

I was confused. He never acted out in anger like that before. And my arm hurt, bad. I could barely keep up with his quick pace as he dragged me behind him.

"Luke, stop."

He said nothing.

"Luke, what are you doing?" I asked as tears rolled down my face.

He finally pulled me into Brooke's sunroom. It was not private at all; the entire room was glass. Everyone could see and hear us. There was no privacy. Everyone could watch my embarrassment unfold. He didn't care. Finally, he let go of my arm, I rubbed where his fingers had dug into my skin.

"What the hell is wrong with you?" he launched into me.

I looked out through the wall of windows and saw everyone staring at us. Mouths open, stunned. I glanced at Brooke by the barbeque, who, to my horror, was standing there with a small smile.

My face was drenched in tears by that point.

"Wh-wh-why are you doing this?" I asked, my voice shaking.

"WHY AM I DOING THIS?" he boomed. "Because ever since Larkin got back, you have turned into a massive bitch." His face was red, his eyes were wide, his mouth was tight as he formed his words. He pulled his hand through his hair, then began to pace. "Yes, I was watching the game in the stands when she was injured. Yes, I saw it happen. Yes, I missed her . . . for so long."

"Luke, please stop." I started to hyperventilate.

"And, YES, I DO still have feelings for her."

I said nothing.

He said nothing.

He just stood there watching me cry.

"And you know what the thing is? The way you're acting makes me want her more."

I flopped down on the floor, grasping my knees into my chest, sobbing. The weight of gravity was pushing me into the ground. I was hoping to be swallowed whole, to drown in concrete. I felt completely exposed in my bikini. The floor was cold against my feet and butt as I sat there grasping my thighs. The air conditioning made me shiver. My tears were hitting my knees. I cradled my head in between my forearms and grasped the hair on the back of my head.

"Why can't you just be nice?" he softened his tone. "You have no idea what she's been through. How can you be so cruel to someone that is so sick?" He knelt down next to me, changing his entire demeanor.

"Yeah, what about me? WHAT ABOUT ME?" Suddenly, I was the one yelling, but not out of anger. I felt nothing but fear and embarrassment. Fear, because I felt like everything was slipping away from me. Like everything I loved was so close, but I couldn't touch it. Like every time I reached out, our relationship moved further away. I was stuck there crying on the floor in front of him, in front of everyone, exposed, and he didn't care. The thought flashed through my mind; my mom had been right all along, I was unlovable. I didn't deserve love.

"You just don't understand what she's been through," Luke said as he pleaded with me to somehow understand what he was saying.

I looked up at him and repeated my question.

"What about me? What about what I've been through. You have no idea," I cried out to him, wiping my tears, and trying to catch my breath. "You're with me every day, but you have no idea what I deal with. You don't really KNOW me." I stopped to take another choppy breath, but I never took my eyes off of his, "You kiss me, you sleep with me, you call me your girlfriend, but you don't KNOW me." I wiped the snot from my nose with the back of my hand. "I have defiled myself for YOU!" He leaned in closer to me, but I tried to push him away. "She's not the only person in the world that has been through shit!"

I slowly got up, wiped my tears, and begin to gather myself. I paced for a bit shaking my hands to warm up.

"Can you hand me a towel please?" I asked, pointing to a blue towel on the table near us.

He silently handed it to me while I regained my composure. I wrapped it around my body and left the sunroom, leaving him behind. No one said a word. They just watched me as I walked to the tan pool chair that held my bag. I forced myself to go cold emotionally, to not care what everyone thought as they watched me pick up my bag and silently walk to the gate to leave.

"Reagan!" Izzy chased after me. She reached me, but I pushed her away and walked without saying a word.

. 27 .

Larkin

My alarm clock's buzz broke me from my trance. I should have felt tired from staying up all night writing my memoir, but I didn't. I might as well have been sleeping because the dreams and the memoir were the same as what happened to me two years ago. That moment was always on replay during my dreams. The memory of the sweet-smelling grass mixed with the stench of sweat. The sound of the other player running. There was nothing out of the ordinary, except that it seemed to happen in slow-motion. I dove to block the ball from going into the goal, reaching above my head, and grabbed it. My hands held onto it tightly. Even with my arms outstretched, I had a firm grasp. The other player pulled her leg back to kick just as my head hit the ground . . . then blackness.

Not only did I hit my head when I fell, but I was also kicked, which made my head bounce off the goal post. The last thing I remembered, as I was blacking out, was the warm metallic taste of blood coming from my mouth, the prickling of the grass, and a player falling over me. Then I woke up in a hospital bed with nauseating pain. The scent of disinfectant was overwhelming. The relentless beeping of the heart monitor was searing my brain with each intensifying beep.

Part of me thought if I wrote it, I would stop dreaming about it. Like, if I got it on paper, it would leave my mind and give me peace. I woke up in a cold sweat every morning, shocked, feeling as if I had just been kicked. It was worse when I was still stuck in bed, in the dark. I would wake up feeling as if I was trapped beneath the darkness of the ocean, drowning. Never to see light again.

What I relived in my nightmares was what I was reliving in my memoir for Mr. Parson's class.

I could smell the muffins my mother was making downstairs. I felt nauseated at the thought of being forced to eat them. I needed to get out of the house without my mother forcing me to eat.

My brothers were already fighting. The noise was deafening, as usual. I felt irritated. I decided to jump in the shower and try to gather myself. If nothing else, I wouldn't be able to smell the muffins in the shower.

I had a few moments of solace, with the hot water hitting my shoulders and my mango scented shampoo rejuvenating me again. I escaped the smell of food and the constant pressure to eat.

Then my brothers started pounding on the bathroom door.

"Larkin, what's taking you so long!" my youngest brother yelled.

Sigh.

"Larkin, seriously, we're going to miss the bus. COME ON!"

"Larkin, this is your mother. You need to hurry; the boys have to brush their teeth."

"FINE!" I really wanted . . . no, I needed my own bathroom. I got the last bit of conditioner out of my hair, turned off the water, wrapped a warm towel around my body, and left the bathroom. I stomped past everyone as they all bum rushed at one time to get into the bathroom. Wrapped in my towel, I went to my bedroom, closed the door, and locked it. I sat on my bed waiting for them to leave.

I finally heard the door open followed by my brothers' voices in the driveway. They were obviously fighting. My mom didn't come upstairs to mention breakfast, or anything. They were just gone. I didn't have to eat! I felt relieved.

Knowing I had to put something in my stomach, I went down to our kitchen, still in my towel. I started some water for tea and grabbed a rice cake. I sat and quietly checking the notifications on my phone while my kettle slowly boiled. Then I heard a knock at the door. I was still in my towel. I couldn't decide if I should open the door or run and hide. So, I quietly got up, walked to the kitchen window, and carefully pushed the curtain aside bit by bit.

It was Luke. I didn't know what to do. Open the door? Not open the door? Despite the fact that I was in towel, and with my judgement lacking, I opened the door, just a crack.

"I'm not dressed yet. You need to stay at least five feet away from me at all times. Do you agree?"

I heard a chuckle, "I agree."

"I mean it, Luke."

"I do solemnly swear that I will stay at least five feet away from you at all times."

"And you will not touch me," I said pointing at him.

"I do solemnly swear to not touch you while you are in the towel," he responded mischievously.

"No, Luke. You must promise not to touch me. Period."

"I do solemnly promise not to touch you because you have your period," he laughed.

"Jerk!" I opened the door. "Eyes on my face!" Then I added, "And, by the way, the period comment was uncalled for."

"Yes, Ma'am. And, sorry."

"Sit in the living room, I'll go get dressed."

"You know I've seen you in less."

I couldn't believe he said that. He was referring to a bathing suit, he'd never seen me in less than a bathing suit.

"That's not the point, Luke." I huffed and walked from the room. Once I was out of earshot, I ran up the stairs as quickly as possible to get dressed.

When I got to my room, I texted him.

***

Larkin: What are you doing here?

Luke: I thought I would drive you to school.

Larkin: What? I do own my own car, you know.

Luke: My car is better.

Larkin: Touche.

Larkin: What about Reagan?

Luke: What about her?

Luke: Good Lord woman, just get dressed. You worry too much.

Larkin: Fine.

***

I couldn't believe he was doing this, especially after what happened at the pool party.

I rushed around my room to find clothes, threw on some makeup, and put my hair up into a wet messy bun. Then, I hopped down the steps and burst into the living room as if I were the star he had been waiting for.

"And I'm dressed."

BEEEEEEEEEEPPPP

My kettle startled me. I turned quickly and ran out of the room to the kitchen. I could hear him laughing the entire way. I was glad my state could make him laugh, after all he was the cause of it.

I yelled into the living room, "Want some black tea?'

"No, thank you."

I poured myself a mug and took it and my rice cake into the living room.

"So, what's up with the Uber service from you?" I questioned him.

"I just thought it would be a good way for us to talk," he shrugged.

"What do you want to talk about? The pool party? Me making an ass out of myself?"

"We should probably talk on the drive, since we have to be there in about," he looked at his watch, "15 minutes."

"Right." I wish he would have called first.

"We gotta go. Come on," he said as he rushed me with a smile and chuckle in his voice.

"Fine!" I snapped back.

It was perfect for me. I could put the rice cake down so he wouldn't notice I didn't eat it. I was able to get a few bites, so I thought I would be okay for the day.

"Alrighty then, let me just put this mug in the sink, grab my backpack, and we'll go. You know, your Uber rating is going to go down for rudeness."

"I'll take that chance," he said smugly.

This fake back-and-forth bickering was the exact reason we had made such a great couple. We were light and fun. And he was hot. So, I decided to enjoy the moment. But there has to be more to a relationship than fun and good looks. I needed to be able to trust him, and that was something I couldn't do.

We grabbed our stuff and walked out into the already humid morning air. I jumped into his blue Wrangler; top off, of course. Before he started the engine, he looked at me and smiled. It was obvious he was thinking about something. His engine started with a loud gruff that startled me.

"If I were single, what would happen?" he asked as he backed out of my driveway.

"I honestly don't know. I can't answer that right now."

"I wish you could. I'm trying to make a big decision."

"Honestly, I'm surprised that you ever started dating her to begin with."

He looked directly into my eyes. "I thought I would never see you again."

"That was a choice you made."

"It's more complicated than that."

"Okay, well, I don't know what to tell you. With everything going on, I just don't know where my head is right now," I replied.

"Can I kiss you again?" he asked.

I couldn't believe he asked that.

"Wow! No! First, you have a girlfriend. Second, your girlfriend wants me dead." I looked at him like he had three heads. He signaled and pulled onto the road. We sat in silence for a bit. That silence was hard; it was lonely. I just wanted to feel close to someone. Anyone.

There was a darkness inside of me no one could understand, and I could never let anyone see it. I had to hide it. No one could hurt me if I made sure I was alone. At the same time, I was terrified of being alone. My walls were slowly crumbling. I just wanted to be loved, but I was so very afraid of it.

"How do you feel being back?" Luke asked, shaking me from my thoughts. "Do you think you'll play soccer again?"

"I can't. Soccer is over for me." I answered as I studied my fingers. The heaviness of that statement hurt.

"I'm sorry. It was your life."

I looked at him and felt myself getting red. My eyes started to well up with tears. I bit my lip and tried to stop myself from crying.

"I probably shouldn't have brought that up," he said sheepishly.

"No, probably not," I replied softly while looking out the window.

He reached and grabbed my hand, which was resting comfortably on my knee. "I hope you know I care."

"Right . . . Well . . . Thank you," I replied, still looking out the window. I was trying not to engage. I was trying to hide my tears. "Actually, I am going to coach a U8 girls' team, but I won't ever play again. At least it's something."

We rode the rest of the way holding hands. Having human contact was actually nice. But it made me realize just how lonely I had become. I didn't want him to let go, but I knew he had to. This was wrong. I couldn't hold it in any longer. I started crying, grieving for what I had lost. Luke glanced at me and tightened his grip.

He found an abandoned parking lot and pulled in, parking his car in the most remote spot possible. "Larkin, what's going on?"

It was hard to answer him, so I didn't. I could control the tears if I stayed silent. I just looked into his eyes without saying anything. He reached up and started stroking my cheek. It was what he always used to do. It felt like home. I needed someone other than my parents to show they cared.

I decided to welcome the gesture. My hand reached up and touched his hand. I let out a deep sigh. He leaned over and slowly kissed my tear stained eye. His breath was warm and smelled like toothpaste. He kissed my cheek where my tears were falling. I found it hard to slow my breath as he looked into my eyes and kissed my other eye. I leaned into him. He kissed my cheek again.

"I don't know what's going on, but I'll be here when you are ready to talk," he whispered into my ear.

Shivers were raging up and down my neck and back. He looked into my eyes for a moment, then as if all at once, we both leaned in forcefully to a kiss. It completely took my breath away. Luke had always been a spectacular kisser, not that I had ever kissed anyone else at that point, to know any differently. He reached up and put his right hand behind my head, his fingers weaving through my hair, and pulled me in tighter as the kiss became heavier.

The image of Reagan popped into my mind. I pulled my arms away from him and slightly pushed him away. He loosened his grip and backed up. We were both out of breath, and his cheeks were flushed wet from my tears. With his forehead resting on mine, he looked at me even more deeply.

"Okay, I'll stop," he whispered.

He backed up and leaned against his seat, trying to calm his breath. He put his blinker on and pulled out onto the road. I looked out my window, but saw nothing, I was too deep in my own thoughts to see anything of worth in the world outside of his Jeep. Luke reached over to me and grabbed my hand. I took a deep breath. His hand felt hot as his thumb ran back and forth over mine. We sat in complete silence. I wanted to ask him about Reagan, but I didn't. I decided to enjoy the moment. I didn't think it would happen again. I couldn't let it happen again.

We pulled into the school parking lot, which was strangely empty. He didn't park in his usual spot, presumably so Reagan wouldn't see that I was in the car with him.

"Where do we go from here?" he asked in a gentle hushed tone.

"You have to make your own decision on this. Don't come back to me because you feel sorry for me," I replied.

"That's not what that kiss was. I promise."

"Still though. Don't make it because of me."

He looked at me once more, leaned in and gave me a small kiss on the lips, then lingered there for a bit. His hot breath giving me the shivers again.

"Okay, let's face the world," he said and got out of the Jeep.

I wasn't ready to "face the world" at that moment, but I got out of the car and followed him into the building. We glanced at each other as we parted ways.

I walked directly to the bathroom.

. 28 .

Reagan

I sat in Izzy's gold Prius, fuming. She was talking to me the entire time, but I had no idea what she was saying. I wasn't listening. Honestly? I just wanted her to shut up for once.

I looked out the window at the passing houses, hoping to see Luke's Jeep. No such luck. My heart started to twist. He hadn't talked to me since the pool party. He hadn't even told me he wasn't going to pick me up for school that morning. He just didn't show up. We hadn't broken up, but he was slipping through my fingers. My stomach was in knots thinking about walking the halls of the school after the display on Saturday. I was sure he was going to break up with me. I was sure that day would be the day I lost everything. The day it all would fall apart.

I felt like nothing without him. But it was only a matter of time. None of it had been mine to begin with. I knew that. I wasn't stupid.

I turned Izzy's air vents toward me so the cool air could hit me in the face. I took the air deeply into my lungs and closed my eyes as my hair blew away from my face.

"I think their offense is strong. The ball may be hitting you hard." Izzy just kept talking.

"Yeah," I responded absentmindedly.

"Okay, what's wrong? You are usually all-over game talk." She looked at me quickly, then turned her eyes back onto the road.

"It's nothing. I'm just thinking." *I didn't need any more drama.*

"Are you still thinking about what happened at the party?"

We stopped for a school bus, I watched mothers waving goodbye to their small children. The pudgy cheeked kids were waving back with tiny hands. I don't remember ever having a moment like that with my mom. I remember my neighbor walking me to the bus stop. She certainly never waved goodbye to me.

"Reagan! What's going on? You aren't listening to me at all, are you?"

"Oh, sorry. I'm just think . . ." I saw Luke's Jeep pull out in front of us. Someone was in there with him.

"Is that?"

"Yeah," I said with a solemn tone. I had a feeling I knew who was there with him. I wasn't mad, I just felt overwhelming sadness.

"Wait. I thought I was picking you up because he was sick or something." She looked at me quizzically.

"He hasn't talked to me since Saturday," my voice was low. "He didn't tell me he wasn't picking me up."

"Wait, he didn't text you or anything?"

"No."

"Shit," she said, slamming her hand on her steering wheel. She was pissed, but I wasn't. I was cold.

"Is that her in the passenger's side?" she asked.

"I don't know," I said lazily.

"CARE! Care, right now!" she yelled. "Snap out of it!"

We pulled into the school parking lot. It felt empty. I saw Luke's Jeep at the end of the lot, far away from where he usually parked. I didn't have the energy to try to figure it out at that moment.

Izzy turned to me. "Okay, whatever happened Saturday, it was bad. I hated seeing you like that," she continued as I turned to look at her, "Whatever he said to you? He's an ass!"

I said nothing. I just sat looking out the window toward Luke's Jeep. They weren't getting out, so I didn't know for sure if it was her. People started pulling in, so my view was blocked a little bit. But I could tell he was leaning in toward whoever was in there with him.

"Okay, look. Let's go in and deal with whatever today brings. I promise. We won't let her win," she said to me.

"She's already won," I replied.

"NO! No! Stop!" she opened her door. "Walk across that parking lot like the bad ass bitch I know you are. Do not look sad. Look proud. Done. Let's do this."

I didn't feel like it. I wished I could have just melted into my seat. I wished everyone who saw the fight never saw me again. I didn't feel like I would survive the day. I couldn't move.

"Get the hell out of the car and do this! Right now," she growled at me.

"FINE!" I snapped back. She was right though; I needed to stop this and get out of the car.

I took a deep breath and stepped out. I told myself to look straight ahead and not look over towards Luke's Jeep.

I couldn't fight the urge. I looked to my right, past the cars, past my friends, and past the other students. Beyond them, all I saw was Luke walking toward the door to the side entrance of the school with Larkin following a few steps behind. He had a shitty grin on his face, and she had her head down, not looking up at all. There was one thing I could see from a mile away, that was that her face was bright red. She was blushing. Once I noticed the blushing virgin, I knew exactly why he was grinning.

I hated him!

I hated her!

Done! I was done! I was so done!

. 29 .

Larkin

Thank God no one was in the bathroom. The strong scent of bleach from the nighttime cleaning crew was heavy in the air. The bright lights were strong and blinding. I was feeling dizzy. I bent over, then leaned against the white tiled wall and put my arms on my thighs for stability. My vision started to go fuzzy and my heart started feeling like it was going to beat out of my chest. I couldn't catch my breath. I sat down on the cold, hard floor. There was a dead roach about three feet in front of me. I stared at it while a wave of despair and panic fell over me. All I could think was that I was that roach. Dead and partially squashed.

I grew dizzier and dizzier. I put my head down on my knees and cradled myself. My heart felt like it was twisting, and my chest felt like a weight was on top of it, pushing into me.

I looked at the roach again and thought everyone would be better off without me. I kept thinking about all the problems I created for everyone. I caused medical debt. I made my mother cry. My friends didn't even come to visit me because I wasn't worth it. I wasn't worth the drama I brought.

I reconsidered. I wasn't like the roach at all. The roach was free, and I was caged. He was free from worry and fear. He was free from second guessing every move. I felt like I was no one. I was the fool. Everything was my fault. Everything.

My breathing was getting harder as if my rib cage was closing in on my lungs and my ribs felt like they were cracking one by one with each breath.

My mind flipped like a switch toward Luke. A Keats quote flashed through my mind, *"Touch has a memory."* I would lie if I said I didn't think about every other moment we had. All of the memories came flooding back. We were electric.

When we were together, we had so much passion, but we never took it past kissing. It was perfect, and at the same time, innocent. We got together after he shot the winning goal for his team to win a tournament. I remember running up and throwing my arms around him. He told me he wanted me to be his. We had been friends for a while, but that moment was what started everything for us. But then he moved on . . . with Reagan. And there I was, shrinking. He grew while I laid in the dark.

I fully realized how depressed I had become. I refused to eat. I was in a constant state of panic. And I felt alone. When Luke and I were together, and I was a goalie? I had no idea that wouldn't last forever. I had no idea it could all go away so quickly, in the blink of an eye. You never know what's going to happen next. That was what scared me so much. I was there, then I wasn't. My life stopped, and theirs kept going. They kept living. Everything he should have done with me, was done with her. Reagan stepped into my life seamlessly. There I was, demanding my life back from her. She'd had it for two years. Who was I to suddenly arrive back and take it away from her? Luke was my first love, but she had him now.

Suddenly, my breathing became worse. I couldn't catch my breath. My head was swimming. *What had I done?*

Tears were flowing freely and dripping onto the floor. I stared at the roach. It didn't look dead, it looked at peace.

I wondered if anyone would care if I disappeared. I mean, I knew they'd cry at my funeral, sure. But how long before they began to forget about me? How long until I was just a photo at a high school reunion? The bell rang, knocking me out of my thoughts. Some ninth graders came running in, not noticing me at all. As I sat there staring at the peaceful dead roach, a girl in pink flip flops stepped on it. She didn't even realize she did it, she just did. He was completely squashed, guts oozing everywhere and probably on the bottom of her flip-flop too. She didn't care. No one did.

The girls were laughing and talking about their dates for the weekend. They put on lipstick, then took a few selfies. All of this while I sat balled up on the floor. They didn't even notice me there at all. They didn't notice the bug guts all over floor that now resembled a gory horror scene. They were completely in their own worlds. *How dare they not notice?*

I got up, startling them, and walked to a sink to wash my face. Once again, I had started my day with a panic attack. Once again, I looked like a pile of shit. Once again, I had to fix my makeup and my hair, and go on as if nothing had happened. I'm not talking about the kiss, I'm talking about the fact that I had those horrible panic attacks, and I tried so hard to hide them. It never worked, but I tried. I didn't want them to see what was going on inside my mind. I opened my bag and rustled around trying to find my makeup kit. I had to make myself look normal—as if normal was possible for me. I perfected my winged eyeliner, wisped my mascara, swept on some bronzer, and straightened the fly away hair back into the bun. I stood staring at my reflection. I did not recognize who I had become.

The girls next to me were still loud, still so happy. They had no idea of the wreck that stood next to them. I turned, put everything away, and left the restroom, leaving my squashed roach friend behind.

I eulogized him in my mind as I walked.

. 30 .

Reagan

My step was much quicker. They saw me coming and they got out of my way. Everyone knew something was about to go down; they knew I was pissed, but they didn't know why. One girl, with black hair and a pile of books in her hands, jumped out of my path so quickly she dropped everything in her arms. I stepped over the books like the bitch I was, like the bitch they knew I was. Like the bitch everyone wanted me to be.

Luke was at his locker like as expected, surrounded by three of his friends. He didn't see me coming. As I walked up behind him, his friends stopped laughing. I grabbed his shoulder and turned him around with more force than I ever used with another human being.

"What the FUCK?" he said as my fingers dug into his shoulder.

"Yeah, WHAT THE FUCK?" I said with force in my voice. "What the hell is your problem?"

I stood with one hand on my hip, my head cocked to the side, lips pursed together, and eyes tightly holding his like some sort of dark witch power.

"You kissed her! Didn't you?" I accused more than I asked.

He laughed, which just infuriated me more. "Who?"

"Don't play with me." I took my pointer finger and pushed him in the chest with it. "You made me look like an idiot in front of everyone at Brooke's. BUT I was RIGHT, wasn't I?"

"You're acting crazy. Stop. NOW."

He couldn't hold his temper much longer. I could tell by his voice.

"Crazy? I'm Crazy? You had me on the floor crying in front of everyone this Saturday, or have you forgotten?"

"Right, we are done here," he said to me with a low voice and clenched jaw.

"Whatever, dick!" I snapped.

He walked away, knocking into my side as he passed.

I looked around. Everyone was staring at me. No one moved. The hallway was silent. I didn't care. I walked past all of them with my head held high. Izzy, who was watching from afar, walked over and took her place beside me. Together we walked down the hallway like we owned it.

"Felt good, didn't it?" she asked me.

"Yeah."

"She's back, ladies and gentlemen," Izzy proclaimed loudly for all to hear.

. 31 .

Larkin

I walked out into the busy hallway. Everything was quiet. They all looked shocked. I couldn't figure out what was going on.

I wasn't even thinking about the kiss anymore. The mass of students near me really triggered my anxiety. All I could think about was navigating the hallway without breaking down. It took all my energy to hold it together, especially with what had happened at the pool party and then this morning.

As I passed through the hall, I felt myself falling back into my old pattern of making myself as small as possible, so no one would notice me. I whispered to myself: *Please don't talk to me, please don't talk to me, please don't talk to me.* Over and over again.

Suddenly, I froze. People were walking past me. Everything felt like it was in slow motion.

Reagan was standing in front of Luke. She looked as if she was going to murder him. I bit my lip to stop myself from freaking out. My locker was about ten down from where they were standing. I couldn't go there; I knew exactly what they were arguing about. My stomach started hurting, my vision dimmed, and it was harder to breathe.

Looking in the opposite direction for an escape, I saw Marco. He was by himself, searching for something in his backpack and not noticing the scene that was unfolding. I quickly walked towards him as if he was my safety.

I reached Marco and stood next to him with my head down, saying nothing. I could feel everyone's eyes on me. They knew who Luke and Reagan were fighting about. Marco didn't; he didn't have a clue. He didn't even notice everyone staring at me. He couldn't have cared less.

"Philip Larkin, how are you, friend?" He hadn't really looked at me yet, he was still digging through in his bag.

"Hi!" I said quickly. He looked at me. I glanced away, but not before he saw that my eyes were bright red.

"Something tells me you aren't okay. What's up?" he looked concerned.

"Nothing. Let's just get out of here," I said, looking at the floor.

"Ah, yes. The unfortunately fucked up Larkin. My dear, I'm here. I'm here for whatever you need," he bowed his head to me as an act of weird chivalry. "I was hoping you would run into me today, literally. I haven't dropped a thing in days."

I couldn't help but laugh. The laughing helped; the darkness started to go away. I could breathe better. I was thankful for the fact that he was unaware of Luke and Reagan's fight, and that it was happening so close to where we stood. He had no idea that I was going to have to avoid both Luke and Reagan, none of that mattered to him. He was just happy to see me. God, I was a mess.

"You are odd! I promise I'll run into you next time."

"Pinky promise?" he held out his pinky.

I wrapped my pinky around his. "Pinky promise." We both nodded and smiled.

I started to hear yelling. I had to get out of there.

"Lunch again today, Phil?"

"Yes, please?" I said in a rushed tone

"Dare I say that it's a date?"

I tried not to laugh. My life hung in the balance at that moment. I had to get out of that hallway.

"It's a pretty pathetic date if you ask me. I think you could do better," I replied.

"True. Okay, it's not a date, but it's something," he said.

"Yes, it's something. Let's get going. We don't want to be late."
COME ON! LET'S GO!!!!

"To somethings," he said as he held out his hand to shake mine.

Luke walked past me, not noticing I was there. I told myself to not focus on him, to not even look at him.

"This is me," I said to him when we reached my history classroom.

I apprehensively entered the room knowing Luke would be waiting for me.

I walked down the aisle while others sat staring at me, probably wondering if I was going to take my usual seat in back of him. I did; I sat where I normally did. I thought it would draw attention if I sat somewhere else.

There's something powerful about the sense of smell. It overtakes you. It makes you forget the bad and brings you to a place of joy. His scent was like that for me. It overpowered me in a good way, or maybe it was a bad way. As I took my seat, my brain went to other places, which made me realize I needed to stay away from him.

Brooke came into classroom. She gave Luke a noticeable stare of death as she walked past him, then threw her backpack down and flopped into her seat.

"Hey, girlfriend!" she said in typical Brooke fashion.

I wasn't sure what she was going to say after what had happened at her party.

"Mornin'," I said in a small voice.

"Are you okay? You left my party quickly. I texted you, but you didn't answer." She looked at me pleadingly.

Truth be told, I had avoided clicking on her message. I was just too embarrassed after running out of her party the way I did.

"Sorry, I just needed some time alone." I needed to say something, so she wasn't left wondering about what happened. If she wondered, she'd ask questions. "Wanna go to Juice and Java again today?" I asked, knowing she had soccer practice. I wanted to spend time with her, I really did. I just, well, I just needed to figure myself out, especially where it pertained to Luke.

"Sorry," she frowned and shook her head back and forth, "soccer practices are happening again, so it might be a little while. You should come to our next game!"

"I'm not ready yet."

"Sorry, I know it's hard," she looked down at her fingers.

Luke turned to me.

"So, how ya doin?" he asked.

Still looking at Brooke, I answered him. "I'm okay." Then I slowly turned my head to him, looked him dead in the eye, and said, "How's Reagan?"

"Things will be tough for her, starting tonight," he said, then took another deep breath. "I feel bad for her, I really do. But I can't be with her anymore."

"I saw the argument." I kept looking at him. "This isn't worth it for you."

"Baby, don't get like that. You know what's going on."

"I do, and I know how she is." I took a deep breath. "I'm the one who's wrong here."

"You have nothing to worry about."

Brooke watched us during the entire conversation. When Luke turned around, she looked at me as if to say "what's going on?" She started scribbling something that notebook of hers. Mrs. Lewis walked in the door as the notebook slapped on my desk.

She had scribbled *What's going on here?* with a big bubble question mark.

I scribbled back, *Honestly, I don't know.* I shrugged as I handed it back to her. She wrote furiously and slid it back to me.

Did something happen between the two of you?

Maybe . . . I don't know.

She must not have seen the argument.

We both looked forward. She began taking notes on what Mrs. Lewis had on the smartboard while I stared at the back of Luke's head, smelling the scent of soap coming off of him. Less than 45 minutes before, we were kissing. Less than 30 minutes ago, I was completely freaking out on the floor of the restroom.

The bell startled me out of my thoughts. It didn't cause a panic attack, but I did jump. Brooke looked at me and laughed a bit.

"I'll see you later, 'kay?" she said as she packed her bag.

"Absolutely!"

She got up to leave the room with everyone else. Luke and I were the only ones left.

He turned to me, "You saw the fight?"

"Of course. The only person who missed it was Brooke, apparently," I said with a shrug. "How could I miss it?"

"A lot happened this morning," he nodded. "I know this is hard." He hung his head a bit and tilted his eyes toward me, "I'm sorry."

As we got out of our seats, he came close to me and wrapped his arms around me to pull me in for a strong, tight hug.

"Okay, please. Don't break my heart here," I pleaded. "I'm not completely healed, and I'm definitely broken," I said, realizing this was the first time that I had ever said I was broken out loud.

I don't even know why I said it. This was the guy who had a girlfriend. A girlfriend who happened to be everything I hated, and I had told him my darkest secre: that I was broken.

Luke released me and turned to walk out of the classroom. I followed behind, which felt a little strange. He accelerated his pace. Then I spotted her, the Freshman. She was standing there waiting for him. He walked past her, looked at her, and walked on. She looked confused. "Luke!" she called, but he ignored her.

That was when it hit me, he was already cheating on Reagan. This had nothing to do with me. The way that interaction happened, it was obvious something was going on between the two of them.

I felt like an idiot. Worse, at that moment I realized that I was like him. He was cheating on Reagan and I was starting a relationship with Marco while playing this game with Luke. It shook me to me core.

. 32 .

Reagan

I entered English class with a pit in my stomach. It was the first time I'd seen him since our fight. To make it a million times worse, Larkin was in that class. My classmates started filing in, laughing and talking. When they saw me, they went silent. I knew the looks they were giving each other. I had given that look a thousand times before. They had been talking about me.

Larkin came in and quietly sat down. She glanced at me out of the side of her eye. I didn't hide the fact I was looking at her. She didn't dare lift her glance again. She just stared at her fingers.

Coward.

Luke walked in. *Finally.* I sat up straight and watched him. He turned and walked toward Larkin. *Because, of course.* I was putting so much pressure on my pencil that I snapped it in half.

Then I noticed something. He smiled at her, but she didn't even look at him. He actually walked up to her and said something, but she ignored him like he wasn't even there. I couldn't believe it! I laughed to myself, loudly. I couldn't contain it. Everyone heard me. No matter how much I tried. The smirk on my face grew wider by the second.

Everyone started whispering.

Larkin smiled at the door. I looked over to see that she was smiling at that guy, Marco.

He came in the room and flashed a toothy grin as he walked over to her.

"Hey Phil," Marco said to her.

Phil?

He threw his bag down under the desk on the other side of her and sat down facing her. He was obviously flirting, and she was loving it. She laughed at every little thing he did or said. I knew, instantly, that I could use this.

My smirk turned into a huge smile. Luke sat watching the two of them. His knee bounced up and down under his desk, his face grew red, and his knuckles were white from holding onto his pen too tightly.

As the bell rang, I turned my attention to the front of the room where Mr. Parson was already at his desk looking upset, shuffling through the papers we emailed to him over the weekend. He stood up, then sighed deeply. He didn't look happy at all. In fact, he looked downright pissed.

"Class, I was disappointed with your memoirs," he still searching for something among the papers. Finally, he looked up at us, "I can tell none of you took the time to really THINK about the assignment." He stopped speaking for a moment to look around the classroom, then continued, "I wanted to know how this memory changed your life. I didn't want just a play by play of a moment. We went over this in class."

He began to walk around the room, handing back papers in silence. The tension was high. Everyone was sitting straight in their desks, grabbing their papers as they were placed in front of them.

Finally, he broke the silence, "Except for one paper." He put Larkin's paper on her desk. I laughed to myself again. *Of course, she's always the perfect one.*

She looked down at it wide eyed, like she was simultaneously shocked and horrified. Once all the papers were handed out, he went back to the front of the room. "Everyone, I would like to you listen to Larkin's paper," he said with authority.

I couldn't believe it. We had to sit there and listen to her talk about her concussion? She had already been getting all of the attention.

"Um, Paul," Larkin whispered to him.

I had forgotten they were on first name basis. I mean . . . yeah. Of course, her paper was the best. Her dad was Mr. Parson's best friend.

"I . . . I can't . . . I mean . . . I'm not ready," she said, looking downright scared. "I don't want to live in the past, I can't keep revisiting this."

He leaned over and whispered to her, "This is good for you, trust me." He looked at the class and said, "Larkin's memoir is amazing. She took her accident and owned it, showing clearly the effect it had on her life. Just take a listen."

Larkin slowly got out of her seat looking positively terrified. Her hand was shaking. She walked to the front of the room with her head down. Then took a few deep breaths before she looked at Mr. Parson, then to

Marco. When she looked at Marco, I could see Luke shoot him an angry glance. Her hands were still shaking, but she took a deep breath and started reading.

> The heat was unbearable that day, the field soggy from the morning thunderstorm. We had every reason to believe we would win this tournament. We just had to get through this last game. We beat them in the first round. We were a better team, hands down. I don't want to say I was too sure of myself, but I was. I was a damn good goalie, and I had my eye on one thing. That trophy. This Keystone team had nothing on me. I was ready to block everything, and that's exactly what I did. It was a great game, but it was dirty, both in the fact that there was mud everywhere, and in the fact that the Keystone girls were playing rough. I had been knocked around, hard. They were not afraid to throw themselves into me, and the referee was calling nothing.
>
> At the half, we were winning by only one goal. The team started to worry. Coach Toan gave us one of his famous speeches. We were pumped and we were ready. We left the huddle and went back onto the field. We weren't going to go down easily. I would have to play dirty the same way they did. Not my style at all, but it was reality. I had to put away any fear I had and be ready to slam into some girls. It was the only way.
>
> It happened so quickly. As soon as play began, the ball was hurling itself toward me. I was going to have to dive, and I'd have to dive with girls running full speed towards me. Down I went, with arms stretched out to grab the ball and with mud flying everywhere, including in my eyes. I made contact. I pulled it in tightly to my chest. I could feel the thumping on the ground of the other girls barreling towards me. I saw her, Sarah Jensen, a beast of a girl. She pulled her foot back and-

Larkin stopped reading. She looked up blankly. Her hand dropped to her side, letting the papers fall to the floor. A single tear ran down her face. She turned and walked out of the room.

I couldn't believe this was happening, again. She really did get a pass to leave whenever she wanted to. At least this time she wasn't running.

Mr. Parson walked quickly to the door, but before leaving the room he turned and said, "Class, please stay in your seats. Give her space."

Without missing a beat, Marco stood up.

"Sit the hell down, loser, didn't you hear what he just said?" Luke yelled before he, himself, stood up.

"Luke, sit down," I said. "Don't you remember what happened last time?"

He looked at me, frowned, and promptly sat.

Marco continued on his path to the door, but he didn't open it. He just stared out the window. I could hear muffled talking from the hallway, but I couldn't make out what Larkin and Mr. Parson were saying. Everyone in the class looked around shocked.

Marco looked worried. I had never talked to him before then, not even once. But he liked her, and she obviously liked him. I started thinking that maybe she wasn't the threat I had thought she was. I needed to act, I got up and walked over to him.

"You're really worried about her, aren't you?" I asked him.

"I am. She's been through a lot."

"She has." I plastered a fake smile on my face. "It's good she has a friend like you," I said.

"I'm the one feeling lucky. She's got her problems, but who doesn't?" He stopped speaking and glanced at me. "She's special," he said as he went back to looking out the window, watching what was going on between Larkin and Mr. Parson.

"You'd probably be good for her. You seem calm. I think she needs calm."

"Oh, I know I would be good for her. I'm not sure she sees it, though," he said, finally looking at me. "I worry about her. She doesn't eat."

"I haven't noticed that," I said, trying to act like I cared.

"My sister has struggled with anorexia and I see the same things in her," he replied, his eyes cast foreword, staring off at nothing.

Whoa!

"I just have this urge to try to make her life better. I'm not sure why," he said, but I didn't think he was even talking to me anymore. Words were just coming out of his mouth. "She's like a flower. A delicate flower that bruises easily."

"Okay?"

"Like a gardenia. That's the flower, right? The flower that bruises easily?"

"I have no idea," I replied to him. "You should ask her out. You need more time with her," I told him.

"I have some ideas. She just has to know that I really care."

"I'll help you," I told him.

"Are you friends with her?"

"Sure!" I lied.

Larkin and Mr. Parson turned to come back in the classroom, so we quickly returned to our seats.

Luke sat there giving me the evil eye. He had heard everything. It was perfect.

. 33 .

Larkin

I walked out the double doors to the parking lot. The sun was bright, causing my eyes to flinch, and my headache to flare. The pain was piercing. I stopped walking and grabbed my head. The crowd pushed past me without noticing. They had no idea know what was going on. They all had their own problems, trauma, and pains. It always amazed me how alone you can feel in a sea of people.

I grabbed my sunglasses and threw them over my eyes. Everything dimmed giving me a small reprieve from the stabbing pain. I scanned the parking lot, hoping Marco still wanted to drive me home.

I looked for Marco and found him standing next to an old Saturn near the tennis courts. He didn't look happy, but he was waiting for me. I navigated the rows of cars and students to get to him.

"Hey Phil!" he walked toward me with a smile growing. "How are you feeling?" As soon as he reached me, he wrapped his arms around me and held me in a comforting hug.

"I'm okay."

Like a perfect gentleman he took the bag off my back, walked around his car, opened the door, and threw it on the back seat. Then he opened the passenger side door for me.

"So chivalrous."

He bowed from his waist. "My lady."

"Weirdo!" I said with a laugh and a blush.

It didn't matter what mood I was in, he always made me feel lighter.

"Well, you know . . . people are weird."

"Isn't that a Door's song?

He laughed, "Something like that, but I think they said strange instead of weird." I loved that about him, so much obscure information in that brain of his.

"Right, and something about faces in the rain?" I asked.

"And remembering names." We both laughed.

I got in the car. Then he carefully shut the door behind me and walked around the front. I detected a little skip in his step. That little skip made me feel . . . happy . . . safe . . . special in some way. He opened the door on his side, popped in, and shut the door behind him, seemingly all in one move

"So, Phil, really, how are you? I've been worried about you all day."

"To sum it up. It's like . . . it's like if people could see what was going on inside of me. Would they help me, or would they be horrified?"

"Oh, horrified, absolutely," he said with a smirk. "But I'm here to listen. Talk to me, Phil." He held my hand to his heart and then let it go before he turned on the car, put on the air conditioning, and shifted toward me, resting his hand on my arm.

"You see what happens when I talk about it. I'd rather not right now," I whispered.

He took my hand in his.

"I know, but I had to try," he winked at me, put my hand on my lap, then grabbed the steering wheel.

We backed out slowly just as Reagan and her little groupies came out of the school. They all watched me as we drove past. I looked in the mirror and noticed the group of five girls start laughing.

"Ignore them," Marco said as he glanced at me, "they aren't worth the pain."

He was right. It was hard though. I tried not to take things personally, but how could I not?

We drove in silence for most of the ride. It was a welcoming silence. I often thought that if you are comfortable having silence with someone, they are special to you. His heavy words hung over me the entire ride home.

They aren't worth the pain.

I repeated it to myself forcefully, *they aren't worth the pain.*

He pulled up to my house and turned his body toward me the same way he did before, "You okay?"

"Yeah, I think I'm good."

"If you need anything tonight, just text me." He grabbed my hand and squeezed it. "Don't bother with Luke tonight. He's not worth it. All this shit going on? He'll just cause more stress."

He knew. How much did he know?

"I know. Thank you for bringing me home. I'll text you later."

I started to open the door, but he stopped me. He jumped out of the driver's side, ran around the front, and opened my door for me.

"Mi Lady."

"Such chivalry, my Lord."

He bent over to take my hand. I blushed a little bit. I had never been treated this way. As I emerged from the car, he hugged me, very tightly. As if he was holding on for dear life.

He whispered in my ear, "I'll always be here." Then he gave me a light kiss on my cheek. My entire body went weak. I had flutters in my stomach. That was what I had been searching for, someone who promised they would be there for me. He said exactly the right thing. *And honestly? Luke who?*

He continued to hold me tight. I could feel his breath on my neck, which sent me into complete chills. I could feel the thumping of his heart. I had to admit to myself that I was completely attracted to him. He chose that moment to kiss me on my forehead, then backed away.

"Don't forget to text me, okay?" he reminded me.

Stammering a bit, "O-Okay."

I could feel the heat in my cheeks rising. He walked around to the driver's side, got in, and winked at me through the window. Then he drove off. I stood and watched his car go down my street.

I ran into my house, slammed the door behind me, and breathed. I hadn't been expecting any of that. I took another deep breath, but it didn't slow down my shaking. I walked, completely weak in the knees, to the refrigerator and grabbed a water bottle.

. 34 .

Reagan: Heyyy, Larkin

Larkin: Not now

Reagan: No, listen, I noticed how Marco stares at you

Larkin: Ok?

Reagan: You know, he's kinda cute

Larkin: What's your point?

Reagan: I think you should go for it

Larkin: Why in the world are you texting me about this?

Reagan: Just trying to be nice

Larkin: Right, well. Marco is a good friend

Reagan: The way he looks at you? No, it's more than that

Larkin: Reagan, don't worry. After what I saw today, I don't want your boyfriend

Reagan: You saw the fight? It was about you, so don't go there, if you know what's good for you.

Larkin: That's not what I'm talking about. And is that a threat?

Reagan: Then what are you talking about?

Larkin: Nothing, but I think I may be the least of your worries

Reagan: Again, what the hell are you talking about?

Larkin: It's not my place. Oh, and in the future, please don't fake being my friend. I can handle my own love life without you getting involved. I'm not after your man.

Reagan: Whatever

***

Brooke: So, what's going on with Luke?

Larkin: Absolutely nothing

Brooke: It didn't look like nothing

Larkin: Well, NOW it's nothing

Brooke: What in the world are you talking about?

Larkin: He kissed me on the way to school

Brooke: OMG I knew something happened.

Larkin: THEN, it became apparent that he also has something with a freshman.

Brooke: What? Who?

Larkin: I have no idea who she is, but she was waiting for him after history. He walked straight past her and didn't say a word. She looked destroyed. There was something more there than a little girl crush.

Brooke: That redhead?

Larkin: Yeah! You've noticed?

Brooke: Yeah, I've never seen anything strange, but I had a feeling.

Larkin: Yep. Seeing her look at him made me realize what he really is. I'm over it now

Brooke: Wise decision.

. 35 .

Larkin

It was still hot when I left my house. The humidity was pretty drastic, and my body felt like it weighed a ton. I was just slow. I should have stayed in the air conditioning and run on the treadmill, but I wanted to be outside. Luke was still at soccer practice, so I didn't have to worry about running into him. I finally began to realize what a dog he was. I didn't need him, what I needed was to get rid of any lingering feelings I had. Running into him on that jog was not the way to do that.

My feet pounded on the pavement, but I started to feel even more dizzy. It was hard to run in a straight line. The earth felt like it was in a constant state of waviness, like the sidewalk I ran on wasn't stable. I slowed to a walk, trying to get control and to stabilize myself. I had no idea what was happening, but it didn't feel good.

I heard a car honk behind me. As I turned, the world seemed to trail in my vision like I was living in some sort of surrealist Dali painting. It felt like my brain was moving slower than my head. I closed my eyes to try to concentrate on my breathing.

"Larky! Are you okay?"

I turned toward the car. "Huh?" was all I could manage to answer before I lost my footing and stumbled. I couldn't hold myself up any longer. To keep myself from passing out, I knelt down and put my head between my legs just as everything went dark.

I heard a car door slam and felt someone near me. A hand touched my back as I sat there hunched over.

"Larky?" It was Brooke, but I didn't respond. I couldn't. "Larkin! Larkin!"

I took a deep breath. My vision started to come back slowly. The darkness began to clear. My dead legs felt like they were coming back to life.

"Hey, Brooke," I said, breathing loudly. "I'm okay. I think I've just been doing too much." I was still slightly out of breath.

"Here, let me help you. I'm giving you a ride home."

"No . . ." I started to say, before she interrupted.

"No, I am. You have no choice." She helped me get up and in the passenger side of her car. The coolness of her air conditioning helped me come back completely.

"What happened?" she asked.

"I think it's just too hot for me to run. I kind of blacked out a little bit," I replied, a headache searing in my skull.

"That's not good. Let's go get some food and a nice cool drink."

"No. I think I just need to go home."

"Okay, well, we'll just go through the drive through. I want to keep an eye on you a little longer to make sure you're okay. Not to mention, I'm starving."

I had to be honest with myself. I was REALLY hungry. "Okay, yeah." We drove to McDonald's, where she ordered two Big Macs, a large fry, and two large Cokes.

"How do you stay so skinny eating like this?" I asked, it still hurt to talk.

"You remember how tough soccer practices were?"

"Oh, yeah. Of course." I could eat anything back then and not gain an ounce. Actually, I had to eat a lot to keep my weight up.

We started digging into the hot fries the way we always used to after practices. I remember those days well. After every practice we would gorge ourselves on fries. Coach Toan would have been extremely upset with us if he had any idea, luckily, he didn't.

"This feels like the old days, doesn't it?" Brooke asked.

"It totally does. I've missed you."

"You know? We should do this often," she said with a smile.

I mirrored her smile, but inside I felt dread. All I could think about was that she could eat all that because she was getting a lot of exercise. I wasn't. I needed to count the calories, but I was too scared to figure out how much McDonald's would set me back. I couldn't afford this, and the food was making my stomach hurt. But I still ate.

"We totally should!" I replied. I didn't want to hurt her feelings. I was eating way too many fries. I knew it, but I couldn't stop. My energy started to come back, but my stomach was so full that it felt like it was going to explode. I took a big gulp of Coke. More calories. Empty calories.

Brooke turned on the radio and we both started singing loudly. It hurt my head to sing, but I didn't care anymore. For the first time in a long time, I had energy. It really did almost feel like old times. When we got to my neighborhood I started fixating on the calories. The fries and Coke had probably set me back around 2,000 calories in one sitting. The thought of that made me feel nauseated. Good thing I hadn't eaten the Big Mac. When we reached my house, she stretched over to the passenger side and gave me a big hug.

"Try to rest, okay? I don't know what happened back there, but it sure did look scary to me."

"I know. I will."

"Love you, Larkin," she said in a quiet tone. "Take care of yourself. I can't lose you again."

"I will. I promise," I replied back. Her words cut through me.

I gathered my trash and uneaten food and headed inside my house. The smell of the Big Mac was calling me. It consumed me. I couldn't take my mind off of it. I had brought it in intending to throw it away, but I couldn't. I had to eat the rest of my food.

No one was home, so I sat and shoved the Big Mac in my mouth. It felt so good to eat, to feel satiated. That was when my brain started counting the calories I had consumed, against my calorie output.

Remembering that I hadn't finished my run. I started to panic. My heart rate jumped, I began to sweat, and my limbs went numb. I needed to get that food out of me. Right then, right there, nothing else mattered. It hurt my stomach. I felt like a bloated marshmallow. I had worked so hard up until then. I needed to get it out, any way possible.

I ran up the stairs to the bathroom, leaned over the toilet, and shoved my pointer and middle fingers down my throat. My throat started constricting and my stomach heaved. The blood vessels in my head felt like they were going to explode. Nothing happened. I tried it again, this time going further back down in my throat. I could feel the food burn my esophagus. It erupted from my mouth, my stomach spasming. After I stopped puking, I looked inside the toilet. The mush and chunks of what was my food with Brooke made me feel more nauseated. So, I shoved my fingers down my throat one more time.

I gagged and again I felt something rise from the depths of my stomach. It burned worse that time. There was a little bit of food, but also stomach bile. My mouth felt like it was on fire. My face was sweating. My eyes teared. I had never purged before, so I had no idea what to expect. In my mind, I thought I had done what I needed to do. I had crossed a line, but I didn't realize it.

I looked at my reflection in the mirror. I should have been scared at what I had just done, but I wasn't. My hair was stringy. My eyes were red. My cheeks were bright red against pale ghostly white skin. The image of myself should have made me pause, instead I splashed my face with water and stared at my reflection in the mirror.

Hoping a shower would somehow center me again, I turned the water to cold. I still felt queasy in the pit of my stomach. Standing under the water, I let the pressure of the droplets hit my face. The water was freezing. I was freezing. I don't know why I chose to be cold, but it felt like the right thing to do. Maybe my subconscious was trying to shake me out of the mess I was becoming. But I didn't think of any of that. I just stood there, as still as possible . . . freezing.

My teeth chattered; I didn't care. I stood there; not washing, just standing.

Finally, the chattering became so hard that I had to stop the water. But still, I just stood there wishing I wasn't who I was. Wishing I didn't scare my parents. Wishing our medical bills weren't so high because of me. Wishing I didn't get kicked in the head. I felt like a failure, like a drain on my family. I didn't want to be a burden anymore.

. 36 .

Reagan

The moment I heard my mother's car in the driveway, my stomach dropped. I tried to figure out if I should lie and tell her everything was okay. She could always tell when I was lying. Hell, she always thought everything coming out of my mouth was a lie. I had to tell her I might have lost Luke. I was never really sure why my relationship with Luke was so important to her. I mean, our relationship didn't get me into college, didn't get me a scholarship, and it wouldn't find me an internship or a job.

The hair on the back of my neck stood up when I heard her slam the car door. The beeping of the alarm system seared my brain.

I waited.

The front door opened and shut. I heard her sigh the way she always did when she was upset. She was talking to herself, obviously bitching about something, but I couldn't quite hear. She was probably complaining about the dishes in the sink.

I heard her coming up the steps to my bedroom.

My door flew open.

"Didn't think about vacuuming or doing dishes?" she asked me in a huff. "As always, my lazy daughter."

She had been gone for two nights, and this was how she greeted me. I'm not sure why I always thought it would be different. It never was. She just never had the mothering gene.

"Sorry. I've been busy," I replied.

"Sorry isn't good enough," she snapped at me. "Just like your father was, lazy."

"I wouldn't know. I never met him."

"Thank God for small favors," she said before she took a deep breath. "Did you keep to the running plan? You didn't eat fast food, did you?"

"Yes, I ran. No, I didn't eat fast food."

"You still have acne. Are you lying about the food? Fast food causes that, you know."

"I swear."

She looked at me as if she didn't believe me. "Well, a quick check of the trashcan will tell me what you ate."

"Fine, whatever."

"Do not talk to me like that." She raised her voice then quickly changed her tone to sweet, "How's Luke?"

"Well, we aren't really talking right now," I said in a small voice as I watched my mom wheel her suitcase into her bedroom.

Her head whipped around, "What?" She looked at me quizzically, "What do you mean?

"He's been getting closer to Larkin and we had a fight about it," I explained.

"Unbelievable. You can't keep anything good, can you? It's like you actually repel good things." I watched the red creep from her neck to her face. "You know what type of person repels all that is good? Bad people, that's who."

"MOM! What the hell?" I screamed at her. "Why does he matter to you so much? It doesn't make any sense."

"Don't you DARE yell at me ever again," she practically screamed, then stopped and thought for a bit, her voice calm when she spoke again. "There's one thing you have to learn as a woman. It's not what you know, it's who you know. Luke's family is influential and powerful." She pointed her perfectly manicured finger at me, "You need to fix this."

"Mom, did you think I would marry him? Be with him forever?" I started crying. "Why can't you just care about MY feelings?" I looked at her with tears running down my cheeks. "I miss him." I buried my face in my hands.

"Remember, what you do reflects on me. Act accordingly."

"What the hell does that even mean?" I sobbed.

She came to hug me. She hadn't hugged me in at least a year. "I'm sorry, I know you don't understand." She actually apologized; I was so confused. "Look, I got where I am in life because of who I knew. Do you need a reminder that Luke's father holds a huge contract with my firm. Without his support, my firm folds. You already know all this. You need to fix this in any way possible," she explained, running her hand down the hair on my head.

I stopped crying. It was finally clear. I mean, I knew it, but I never really realized it, this wasn't about me. It was about her precious business.

"Plus, the two of you are so cute together. Don't let that weakling take what is rightfully yours."

I started to cry again.

She wiped my tears, "Baby go after what is yours. She's nothing compared to you. She's a weakling who couldn't even handle being a goalie without getting hurt."

"Mom, she got kicked in the he . . ."

"Shh, that doesn't matter. I'm sorry for her, but that doesn't give her the right to come in and take what's yours."

"I think there is this guy, Marco, she's interested in," I said meekly. This was the first time, since I was a little girl, that my mom had stroked my hair. It felt nice. It felt like I had a caring mother for a moment.

"Are you using this information?" she asked.

"Yes, I told him to ask her out."

"Good, that's a good start," she replied. "Now you just have to find a way to make sure Luke stops liking her so much. Can you do that?"

"How?"

"You know how. I raised you to use your femininity to get what you want."

"Mom, I don't want to be that type of woman."

"Oh goodness, you are so naïve," she laughed at me a little bit. Then said, "Just get what is yours."

She stopped comforting me and got up to walk out. Before she left, she turned at the door and said, "Remember, honey, I'm counting on you. You have to get him back . . . for me." Looking me in the eye, she added, "Don't be a disappointment."

. 37 .

Larkin

Marco: Still want to hang out?

Larkin: Absolutely!

Marco: Juice and Java? 7?

The thought of being faced with more food gave me the chills. No, no, I had to think of something else.

Larkin: I have an idea, let's go hang out by the creek, at the kayak dock.

Marco: I really like that idea. I'll pick you up around 6:30.

Larkin: Perfect.

***

I knew full well the trip was risky. We would be alone, something my mom told me never to do on a date. But the thought of spending time with him made me happy. I felt butterflies in my stomach.

I heard the front door slam. "Larkin!" It was my mom.

I walked out into the hallway so that she could hear me yell, "Hey mom!"

"Hey, baby girl, come on down." I had no idea what this was about. I went bounding down the steps with my new-found, Marco inspired, energy. "Hey, mom! What's up?"

She took one look at me and relief washed over her face. "Oh, honey, I'm so glad you are okay."

"Of course, I am," I replied, confused.

"Paul called me at work. He explained what happened and was extremely worried about you."

"Great," I rolled my eyes.

"Don't do that. You have a lot of people that really care about you," my mom pleaded.

"What did he tell you?" I asked.

"He just wants to help. He suggested some things for you. He developed an eating disorder in high school when he was wrestling. So, he's been through all of this. He'd like to take you for dinner this weekend."

"Seriously? How did we not know about this before?" I asked. "Also, don't you find it odd that he wants to go to dinner with me?"

"Really, dear? Don't be like that. He's known you since you were a baby," she pleaded. "You need to learn to take help when it's offered."

"And, of course, he wants to meet for food."

"Stop it."

"Whatever," I said with attitude.

"I'm going to make some shepherd's pie. You'll be here, right?" *Ugh, such a heavy meal!*

"I need you to cut the veggies for the salad," she told me before I could answer her question.

"I'll cut the veggies, but I'm going out to Juice and Java with a friend for dinner," I lied.

"Who are you going with?"

"A boy from Creative Writing. His name is Marco."

"Oh, that's nice. Make sure to eat something. "

"Mom, I will, don't worry. That's why they call it 'dinner.' Also, if you check the trash, you'll notice I had McDonalds with Brooke today."

"Oh, Larkin, that's great. I mean, it's not the healthiest, but at least it's food?"

"Oh yeah, totally," again, I lied. She had no idea I had puked it all up. "I'll go cut those veggies now."

"Do you want to talk about what happened today in class?"

"No, it's okay. It's over now. I've moved on," I talked quickly to try and make her think of something else.

"Oh, I signed you up for group therapy. There's a group that meets at the school after last period. It starts tomorrow."

"What? It starts tomorrow? Where was the warning?" I snapped.

She always did this. She always thought I would feel better just by talking. But I was always talking about it. I was sick of talking about it. I just wanted it all to end.

"I forgot to tell you. Sorry."

"Therapy for what?"

"Eating disorders."

"MOM! What? At school?! I don't need everyone there knowing my business."

"Honey, everyone in the group is going through the same thing. I think it will help you."

"Fine, whatever."

I chopped the lettuce as if I had a death wish for it.

Dinner with Paul and an eating disorder group AT THE SCHOOL? I really thought my mother was trying to make me lose my mind.

. 38 .

Reagan

Running had always cured my anger in the past, so I decided to run my anger out. I couldn't think of a reason why it wouldn't work, so I jumped on the treadmill and quickly worked my way up to a fast pace. Once I got used to the pace, I made the machine go faster. I was always told the only way you could ever get better was by working hard, so I ran hard. Running and I had become close friends over the years, anytime my mother freaked out on me, off to the basement I went to run. Running cleared my head, was my meditation, and made me a calmer person. But running couldn't solve my problems that day.

I was hoping my mom would start to see me for who I was. That I was not a disappointment. That I could fix this. I had to fix it; I had no choice. I needed to become worthy of her love. I was craving her love. I felt like I was losing everything, but if I could get her to appreciate me, that would have made me feel so much better. Luke wouldn't have mattered so much.

I remember the sweat bleeding into my eyes, but I made myself keep them open. The sting of the sweat was a reminder of what I needed to do. This was faster than I had ever sustained before. My heart pumped so loudly I could hear it through the veins in my head. My feet kept the rhythm of my heart rate. I used it as a reminder to not slow down. Never slow down.

I told myself to just keep running.

Through the pain.

Never stop.

The best don't stop.

I never stop.

Without missing a step, I jumped off the treadmill and grabbed my soccer ball to do some rebounds off the wall. I threw the ball against the wall viciously and blocked it as it came back over and over. I needed touches on the ball, so I ignored the stinging in my arms. The ball pounded back and forth, against the wall, against me. Suddenly, it was rebounding back on me so hard that I needed to take a step back. This was unacceptable. My body should be a wall against the ball. My arms started to burn, and my hands stung.

I thought it was perfect. Pain meant I was getting better, stronger. Better and stronger meant I would get approval from my mother. With each throw, I grunted from the sheer force I was using, but the grunting turned to laughter. It was a maniacal, painful, beautiful never-ending laughter. I took all my frustrations, all my anger, out on the ball. It thud as it hit the wall, bounced off the floor, and then back to me. It was like music . . . MY music. It was proof of my strength. I kept telling myself certain things with each throw, almost like a mantra:

Do whatever it takes!
No one is stronger than me!
I am the best!
This is MY time, not hers!
I'm taking it all back, in any way possible.

The intensity of the burn in my muscles pushed me to take action and go to Luke's to win him back. I bolted up to the living room, ran past my mother sitting at her computer, and charged up the stairs to the bedrooms. I needed to look good when I saw him, so I stopped in the bathroom to wash the sweat off my face. I sprayed some dry shampoo in my hair and pulled it into a bun. Then I swiped on some pink lip gloss, the kind that makes your lips look fuller; I needed kissable lips.

I went into my bedroom and grabbed a pair of jeans from my floor, along with a black t-shirt, and threw them on hastily. I was not wasting any more time. I had an important job to do. I threw on the running shoes that were lying haphazardly by the front door. I didn't want to lose my momentum or my nerve, so I moved as quickly as I could. I could still feel the burn of the hard run in my legs, but it didn't slow me down. No, it reminded me of my purpose.

"What are you doing?" my mom asked, looking confused.
For the first time in my life I ignored her and left the house. My mother hadn't cared enough to teach me to drive, so I relied on friends or walked everywhere. But that day I was still on my workout high and decided to run to Luke's. The decision to run should have made me realize I wasn't thinking clearly, but it didn't.

Luke grew up three blocks away from me, so I followed my usual path, passing little kids playing in sprinklers as their dads washed their cars. I ran past classmates who were mowing their lawns and little old ladies that were busy weeding their flower beds. But the only thing on my mind was what I would say to him when I reached his house. As I ran, I pumped my fists, my nails carving into my skin. Getting him back was the important thing, the only thing. I felt like the faster I ran; the more Luke would see that I needed him.

As I approached the blue shuttered house, I slowed my pace. The realization hit me that besides the sheer want of having him back, I still had no idea how I was going to accomplish it. I stopped running and walked his path slowly, trying to compose myself.

The only thing I knew as true was that I had to take back what was mine, what she took from me.

I took the step up to his stoop and stood there for what felt like an eternity. I told myself over and over again to just ring the doorbell. After a while I reached my shaky right hand up to the small round button and pushed. The barking of his husky made me jump. It didn't matter that I had heard the barking every single time that I rang the doorbell for the last two years. Normally, I wouldn't have even noticed it, but I was not in my right mind. I heard footsteps running down the steps. I could tell it was Luke; no one else in the house would run that loudly.

The door opened.

He stood before me wearing only gym shorts.

"Reagan. What are you doing here? Did I miss a text?" he said looking at me quizzically.

"No, I just wanted to talk to you."

With a sigh, he opened the door a little more and stepped aside so I could enter. I tried my hardest to slow down my breathing, to not seem so out of breath. I needed to calm down if I was going to accomplish anything. The last thing I needed was for him to treat me like I was insane. I thought I had it all together. In fact, I was sure I did. But in reality, I was unraveling.

He led me past the hallway of expensive art to his media room. He didn't turn around to look at me even once. He opened the door to the room we had spent most of our time in, usually with our bodies intertwined. Only this time, he turned back to look at me, not with lust in his eyes, but with anger. The overstuffed leather couch and recliners had always felt so comforting in the past, but now they seemed sterile and cold. The wall sized screen that showed the movies we pretended to watch, was playing the Chelsea soccer game. He walked in after me, haphazardly flopped down on the recliner across the room from me, picked up the remote, and focused on the game. The only thing I could do was stand before him as I talked, feeling exposed once again. He wasn't even looking at me; he was looking past me. His full attention on the game. It was like I was a ghost.

"Luke, I'm sorry."

"I'm so sorry." I said, pacing.

I stopped and faced him, "Please, listen to me."

"Just acknowledge me?" I begged.

"Why are you doing this to me, Lukey?"

I had been talking for at least a minute when the commercial came on. He finally looked at me and spoke as if he hadn't heard any of the words I had said.

"What's up?" he asked me lazily. "I have shit to do."

"Luke," I began to stammer. "I- I miss you." Tears began to well up in my eyes, "Luke. I love you." No matter how hard I tried to seem like I was in control, it just wasn't happening. At that moment I knew I had lost him. He was barely even looking at me and, when he did, he looked disgusted "Luke. Plea. . ."

He cut me off. "Just stop. Don't be so pathetic," he said with distaste.

How could he be so cruel? I was standing there in front of him trying to bear my soul. Trying to appeal to him. Showing him what I was feeling. He didn't care. There was nothing I could say, not anymore. Still, I kept trying.

"Luke, she's not right for you." I was pleading. "Stop focusing on her. She likes Marco anyway. You are wasting your time."

He shook his head. "Reagan, this isn't about her. This is about you." He stood up. "You just can't have fun." He used his fingers as a way to count his points, "You're never fun! Everything you do is for show! Even at the lake, when we weren't on showcase for anyone, you still performed for the little kids swimming around us. I mean, WHY?" He began pacing, "All you are is a show. The fact that we have to put on this act in front of our friends is ridiculous. The kisses, smiles, and all the social media photos. All of it is fake."

I interrupted, "What are you talking about? We have plenty of real moments, like when we are here on this couch," I said, pointing to the couch on the other side of the room. "Besides, it's important to project something positive."

"For who? Who are you trying to impress? It's our what? Our BRAND? Branding is fake. Relationships are real." His eyes were wide and the vein in his forehead was popping. "And, by the way, what teenage guy wouldn't sleep with some chick who was throwing herself at him?" His voice was cold, "Don't mistake it for love."

"Some chick? What does that mean?" I asked in a small voice. I couldn't believe he had called me "some chick."

"Never mind." He turned his back toward me and started talking again, "Look, the way you treated Larkin made me realize that you aren't a good person. It changed my view of you, or no . . ." he stopped to run his fingers through his hair. "No, no," he said, pointing at me. "I knew this the whole time, I just didn't care before," he shoved his finger in my face. "Reagan, YOU ARE A BITCH!" he yelled.

"This is 100% Larkin, and you can't say it isn't. You would have never said these things to me before she came back."

"It's not even 10% Larkin," he literally spat his words at me. "God! You are so full of yourself."

"After everything I've done for you?" I couldn't believe the things he was saying to me. He didn't care about me at all. No one cared about me. No one cared about me at all.

"What have you done . . . for me? Please, go ahead, enlighten me," he said as he crossed his arms in front of him.

"I gave myself to you."

"And what does that mean?"

"I slept with you. You were my first."

"You were my first, too. Let's not forget, you were running around with Seth before you were with me. It could have easily been him." He pointed at himself, "That fact doesn't make me special."

I couldn't believe he had said that. I couldn't understand what had changed in our relationship. It was so drastic and sudden. Maybe it wasn't Larkin at all. Had he just been using me? Had he just gone along with my plans so he could get some? I felt like he duped me, like he tricked me into that type of relationship. And, you know what? I was NOT ready for sex when it happened. I did it to keep him. I always did it to keep him. He clearly didn't get that at all.

"I can't believe you just said that to me," I said in a soft whisper. My tears stopped and my eyes went wide.

"Don't act like you were such a perfect little virgin. You weren't. You aren't fooling anyone," he said with a laugh.

That was when I realized there really was nothing more I could say. He had his mind set on Larkin. It was her for certain. He might not have said he didn't want her, but it was clear that he wanted her. He was doing and saying anything he could to get rid of me. There was nothing I could do, and it was obvious. He wanted pure. He thought Larkin was pure. He said it had nothing to do with her, but it did. One hundred percent.

The same rage I felt on the treadmill in my basement returned to fire up inside of me. My heart pumped harder; my hands shook; I turned and left his media room.

I could feel him smiling so I slammed the door. He didn't try to follow me. *Of course, he didn't. Why would he chase me after saying all that?* I ran up his stairs with no more tears in my eyes, just heat. A headache started flaring across my forehead but despite the pain, I ran home. My rage fueled me.

. 39 .

Larkin

Marco's sedan pulled in front of my house. I could feel my heart beating fast, but not like a panic attack, it was excitement. I had spent so much time thinking about going out with him. The possibilities of what could happen were running through my head. For the first time in a long time, I felt excited about the future.

I ran up and gave my mom a quick kiss on the cheek.

"Bye, mom!"

"Wait, don't I get to meet this boy?" she asked.

"Not yet, Mom, I don't want to scare him away so soon," I said with a coy smile and a wink.

"Well, I'm offended." Mom faked offense and let out a little laugh as I threw my arms around in her a tight hug.

"Bye, Mom, love you."

"Love you, too, Lark.

I bounded for the door, completely ready for the next adventure. It was almost like a run to freedom, a run towards a future that I couldn't fully comprehend, towards a someone who could actually see me. I had spent two years wondering what was next, what I was supposed to do, and what I was meant for in this world. I guess that's something you tend to do when you are in bed day and night. Marco represented a change, something new. He was proof there was a future for me, that things could change. I really felt as if he was the answer and I was running toward that answer. I wanted to know what was waiting for me.

I stopped myself before I burst through the front door into the warm, late summer air. I didn't want to seem too excited. That was when my dad saw me.

"Larkin, have a great time."

"I will, Dad."

"If he touches you, I WILL kill him," he pointed at me. "Please relay that message."

"Right." I rolled my eyes prominently so he could see, then smiled widely and walked over to hug him, "Don't worry, Daddy."

Once we broke from our hug, I turned toward the front door. I took that step out of the door and onto my stoop. Marco was standing beside an open passenger side door, holding a small bunch of flowers. I stopped short, looking at him with disbelief. I'd never received flowers before. This was not something Luke had ever done. Not once had Luke ever shown such chivalry. I couldn't help but allow a large smile to spread across my face.

Suddenly, Marco looked like the sexiest man alive. I noticed the way he stood casually, with his arm thrown over the car door. The way he leaned against it with his legs carelessly crossed. And that smile. Oh my God, that smile. The way his white teeth shined, and his eyes crinkled when he smiled made me a little dizzy. But dizzy for a good reason and not because of my injury. I was legitimately swooning.

When I got to him, I felt a little awkward. He bowed as I approached, in the most Marco way ever. But this time, when he stood up straight again, I threw my arms around him. I just couldn't help myself. The feeling of his arms was so completely comfortable, it felt like they were meant to hold me. Simply put, I fit. There was no other way to describe it. WE fit. To add to the swooning, dizzy feeling, he actually leaned down and kissed me on the top of my head. It wasn't much, but it took my breath away. I nestled my head into his chest. I could feel his heart thumping hard and fast. We stood for just a moment before breaking apart. When he looked down into my eyes, it felt as if he was staring into my soul and all at once I felt cared for.

He carefully closed the door after I sat down, then sprang around the front of the car, slid into the driver's side and closed his door. Before starting the car, he looked at me and smiled again. He reached over to squeeze my hand, then sighed as he focused his attention on the car and the road.

Out of the side of my eye I noticed something sitting on the back seat. My heart dropped. It was a picnic basket. A very large basket filled with food. *Crap*. After the McDonald's stop that afternoon there was no way I could eat what was in that basket. Suddenly, I stopped swooning over him and began formulating a plan for getting out of eating.

"Did you bring your creek shoes?" His words shook me from my worrying.

"Absolutely!" I continued to smile at him, careful to not show worry in my face.

We drove through the covered bridge toward the parking lot. Everything was perfect. The trees were beautiful, the sun was low, and the water was rushing. We pulled into the first spot available, next to a group of tubers who had just finished going down the creek. There were families with small children splashing around. Their laughter was barely audible, muffled by the sound of water hitting stones. There was a bunch of adults grilling burgers. The smell wafted into my nostrils making me sick. The smell reminded me of the picnic basket.

"Grab the blanket. I got the basket," he said. I chose a spot next to the water to lay our blanket. I delicately spread it out and sat down to listen to nature. The sound of the water running over rocks was beautiful. The kids splashing and laughing made me so happy that I forgot about the picnic basket for a moment.

One thing I had learned while stuck in bed for two years was to find joy in the little things. The things you wouldn't otherwise notice, those are the things you should pay attention to. I was fully immersed in those little things when he leaned over to kiss me on my cheek. THAT was a big thing.

"Let's swim a bit before we eat. There is only so much sunlight left," he pointed out.

"That's a wonderful idea!" I said.

He held out his arm to help me up. His calloused hands felt rough, but they sent shivers through my spine. We walked to the edge of the water, hand in hand, trying not to slip on the rocks. The cool water ran over my toes. I stood still for a while, enjoying the sensation as Marco waded out right to the middle. The water was rushing past his shirtless waist. It was obvious he worked out . . . a lot. I had no idea. Damn, was he hot! There was much I didn't know about him, apparently.

"Come out with me!" he called to me, laughing.

"Okay, chill! I'm getting there." I threw off my oversized t-shirt, revealing my bathing suit underneath and made my way through the cold water towards him. Suddenly, I plummeted into water above my head. Coldness surrounded me, the current pushing against my body, threatening to send me downstream. I was trying to get back to the top just as Marco's arms wrapped around me and pulled me close to him and held me tight as I gasped for air. I went from being scared to feeling safe and protected in his arms all in the blink of an eye.

"Little bit accident prone?" He laughed with his arms still wrapped around my shaking body, "Are you okay?"

All I could do was tilt my head up and nod yes. I was shivering.

Feeling the cold-water rush against my skin contrasted with the warm arms holding me up. His chin rested on top of my head. All of this was pure heaven. I felt weak, but I'm not sure it was because I almost drowned. It was because he was protecting me from the currents, not only in the creek, but in my life as well.

To me? At that very moment? That was exactly what safety felt like. It was everything I had been missing.

Kayakers paddled silently past us as the once warm air cooled around us. A mother called to her children in the water, calling them in for dinner. Finally, we were alone, still holding onto each other. His arms moved up and down my back, warming me, but giving me chills at the same time.

"Larkin, can I kiss you?" he whispered into my ear. Everything about the moment was perfect. I tilted my face towards him as he looked at me.

"Yes," I whispered back. He leaned over and put his hand gently on my chin. He slowly and delicately placed a small kiss on my lips, then straightened himself to look into my eyes. After a few moments, he leaned in for another longer kiss. A kiss that was hard, yet sweet. Passionate, yet innocent. My mouth opened to his as he pulled me more tightly against his body. I felt as if I was going to be swept away again. This time, not into the depths of the water gasping for air, or into a crowded hallway grasping for doorways to safety, but into the safety of his kiss.

When we finally stopped kissing, he straightened his neck and put another small peck on the top of my head. I leaned my head into his chest and just breathed. I had never felt so comfortable with someone before. The amount of peace I felt was unreal. It was something I had craved for so long.

"Let's go eat something," he said.

My stomach grew tight. "Okay."

We broke our grasp, and he took me by the hand to lead me safely to the shore, avoiding the deep spot that tried to tear me away from him.

Thoughts of eating started making me feel panicked. There was no way I could eat, not after purging myself earlier in the day. My stomach and throat still felt raw. I felt like my legs were going to give out from under me.

"It's getting dark. We should probably just go," I pleaded.

"Nah, there's still at least a half hour of sunlight left. We'll be fine." He smiled at me. "I can drive at night."

We sat on the blanket side by side. He grabbed my hand, then kissed me sweetly on the cheek. I swooned, but I had to keep my composure because I needed to concentrate on finding out a way out of eating. He leaned over and opened the basket, showing a full spread of fruit, cheese, and bread. I sighed in relief. I could do this. I could eat the fruit.

"See? I know what you like." He reached in the basket and handed me a bunch of grapes.

I threw a grape in my mouth. 1.5 calories per grape. I ate another while watching him break off a piece of French bread. He tried to hand me a piece, but I turned it down telling him I was happy with the fruit. He frowned at me.

"Larkin, I need to talk to you about something."

I knew exactly what he was getting ready to say. "Okay?"

"I worry about you." He stopped speaking for a moment. I could tell he was trying to figure out what to say next. "I never see you eat." He looked at me with a troubled look on his face, as if he was afraid of offending me. "Holding on to you, I realized how skinny you are."

My eyes started to water. I tried biting my tongue to stop myself from crying, but it didn't work. I could feel a tear roll down my cheek.

He looked at me deeply, "Please, eat a piece of bread. Just one." He put it in my hand then used the tip of his thumb to wipe away my tear. "You don't have to say what's going on. But just eat this," he kept his palm on my cheek, "for me."

Marco watched my face as I took the bread from his hand. I slowly took a bite while counting the calories. *Slice of French bread, 277 calories.* He smiled as I ate, then handed me a bottle of water. I took a drink. He cut an apple and handed a slice to me. I ate that as well. Then he got a plate and began filling it with cheese, grapes, apple slices, and more bread. I thought it was for the both of us, but it was just for me. When he handed it to me, my stomach dropped. *Sharp cheddar squares, 344 calories. A bunch of grapes, 34 calories. Apple, 94 calories.* And more bread. I quickly did the math in my head, but still I ate. I tried so hard to quiet my mind, to stop calculating and worrying, but I just couldn't make myself. I hid it well though, I smiled at him, and laughed at his jokes. And I ate. I ate everything on my plate. He looked pleased that I had eaten so much.

On the drive home it was hard to think about anything but the calories I had eaten. I tried to figure out how much exercise I would have to do. I hadn't eaten cheese like that in a long time. Besides all the calories, my stomach was not at all happy to have the food. We rode in silence, but as I looked at him in the dark with the full moon's light bouncing off his face, all I could see was beauty. I smiled at the way his mouth turned up at the corners and his cheeks made his eyes have a squint that was ever so small. I forgot about the calories. He was happy. He was happy to be there. He was happy to be there with me. I made him happy. Me! I did that!

We pulled into my driveway. He put the car in park, and turned to me. "Thank you, Larkin."

"For what?" I was confused. He brought me here. All of this was his romantic idea.

"Thank you for sharing this with me," he said sincerely. "This was the perfect evening," he said, then sighed, "I think this may be the best first date in history."

I could feel the heat rise in my cheeks. He noticed the red and laughed just a little bit.

Then he took the back of his hand and ran it along my cheek. I didn't know what to say. "I want this date to end on a sweet note, can I just kiss you on the cheek?" There's no other way to say it, he was taking my breath away.

I simply nodded. I mean, what else could I do? He looked into my eyes, then leaned in and placed his lips lightly on my cheek. He held them there for just a moment, long enough for me to feel his breath, then he backed up.

"Thank you for a wonderful time."

I didn't know what to say, so I just smiled.

"Goodnight," he whispered.

I turned and opened the car door and began to walk up my walkway. I took a deep breath before entering the house. I could feel Marco in the car behind me. He didn't start driving away until he knew I was about to safely go inside. He was the perfect gentleman.

My parents were awake when I got home.

"How'd it go?" my mom asked.

"Very well."

"He didn't touch you, right?" my dad demanded.

"It was nice date, and he was a perfect gentleman," I assured my dad. "I'm just really tired. I'm going to get a shower and go to bed."

I sprinted up the steps and into the bathroom. I wanted to take a shower, but the moment I looked at myself in the mirror, I remembered what I had eaten. Bread and cheese. My breathing became heavier. I knew I needed to get it out of my stomach, all of it. Purging was the only answer I could come up with. I wasn't thinking clearly. I didn't think about the fact that my parents were right downstairs or that my brothers were in the rooms surrounding the bathrooms.

None of this crossed my mind as I knelt down in front of the toilet and put my fingers down my throat. It came up easier than the first time.

There was banging on the door.

"Larky . . . Larky are you okay?" My little brother had heard me. "MOM! MOM! Larky is puking. I think she's sick."

Footsteps.

Knock on the door.

"Larkin? Honey? Are you sick?"

One last uncontrollable heave emptied my stomach.

"Yeah, I just got one of those bad headaches. It made me puke. I'll be fine."

"Okay. Do you need anything?"

"No, I'll just get a shower and go to bed."

"Okay, if it stays this bad, I'll call the school in the morning."

"No, I'll be okay."

I knew she was staying by the door. She wouldn't leave that easily. Knowing my mom, she'd be right outside the door the entire time

"Honey, can you unlock the door? I'm just worried you will fall in the shower," she said.

The truth is, I knew purging was bad for me, but I didn't care. The thought of gaining even one ounce was a constant worry. It terrified me. I knew that what I was doing would hurt my parents. They worried a lot about me. They still do.

Just as predicted, my mom was sitting in the hall beside the bathroom door when I came out.

Not only did I purge, but I lied to her.

. 40 .

Reagan: I want you to know, Luke and I are over.

Larkin: Okay?

Reagan: You came back and he changed. This is all you.

Larkin: Me?

Reagan: We were fine before you decided to come back.

Larkin: Were you?

Reagan: Yes. This is all you.

Larkin: You already said that. I don't want Luke.

Reagan: Whatever. Just watch your back.

Larkin: WTH do you mean? This is the second time you've said that to me.

***

Larkin: I just got a crazy text from Reagan

Brooke: That's not surprising. What did it say?

Larkin: She told me to watch my back.

Brooke: WTH! What does she mean by that? And why?

Larkin: She thinks I'm after Luke

Brooke: I wouldn't worry about her at all. What could she possibly do?

Larkin: It felt like a threat.

Brooke: She hurts you . . . she gets kicked off the team . . . goodbye scholarship.

Larkin: True, okay. I'll stop worrying about it.

Brooke: Good! How'd your date go tonight?

Larkin: I'm falling.

Brooke: Oh shit! Grrrl.

Larkin: We went to the creek by the covered bridge.

Brooke: Creative. Did he kiss you?

Larkin: Well . . . Yes.

Brooke: :) Was it a good kiss?

Larkin: Well . . . Yes.

Larkin: We start student coaching tomorrow, right? What field?

Brooke: Changing the subject? I see how it is. Yeah. The fields at the elementary school. Field nine.

Larkin: Okay. I don't think seven-year-old girls will give me another concussion.

Brooke: It will be fun. I know you can't play, but I'm glad Coach asked us to do this. I'll be happy to be on the field with you again. Wanna go for a run before? I have practice, but what about after that?

Larkin: Yeah. 4? My house? And yes, I'm excited about it. I don't even know where my cleats are.

Brooke: Perfect. But don't worry about the cleats.

***

Marco: Hey. Are you warmed up from the creek yet?

Larkin: Of course. Are you?

Marco: As I can be. Thank you for coming out with me tonight. I'm sorry if I made things awkward while we were eating.

Larkin: It's okay. I like that you care.

Marco: Can I pick you up for school tomorrow?

Larkin: Sure, I'd like that.

Marco: Can I hold your hand in the hallway like a middle schooler?

Larkin: Please do.

Marco: Can I kiss you on the cheek, then look away really quickly because I'm blushing.

Larkin: Cliché. You are such a dork. And I love it. Goodnight.

Marco: till morrow.

***

Luke: I won't be taking you to school tomorrow.

Reagan: Asshole.

Luke: Act like you don't know me from now on.

***

Reagan: Can you bring me to school tomorrow?

Izzy: Sure. No problem.

Reagan: And for the rest of the school year?

Izzy: What's going on?

Reagan: We broke up.

Izzy: Reagan, I'm so sorry.

Reagan: He called me a bitch, a whore, and fake.

Izzy: Oh shit. Do we need a plan for getting back at that asshole?

Reagan: No. I'm too tired to care about him anymore. The things he said . . .

160   Abigail Wild

broke me.

Izzy: Reagan. He's just one guy. No one believes any of those things he said about you. He doesn't even believe them. Tomorrow is a new day; we are going to crush it.

Reagan: Thanks. I have to sleep.

Izzy: I'll be there in the morning.

***

Izzy: What the ACTUAL fuck?

Luke: Just shut up. Delete this number from your phone. Don't even think of coming for me. I know how you and Reagan are. Don't mess with me, you will lose.

Izzy: Asshole. You are deleted. I feel sorry for you.

Luke: Ooooookay.

***

Coach: Larkin! You're still coming to coach tomorrow, right?

Larkin: Yes! I'm excited!

Coach: Great! It will be good to have you back on the field. Coaching little girls will be perfect for you. Glad to have you back.

. 41 .

Reagan

All that kept going through my mind was that Larkin had ruined my life. I mean, she had ruined everything I had become. Sure, her injury meant I could have everything I wanted, like Luke and the first-string goalie position, but the point is that it all became mine. Then she showed up and it all started to go away. Everything I had worked so hard for. Hell, even coach was getting her on the field again. I could have coached the 8-year olds! He hadn't even asked me. I wanted her gone and I would have stopped at nothing to have her disappear again.

I knew she was freakishly obsessed with running and I knew her route. I overheard Brooke tell Izzy she would be running with Larkin after practice. I didn't have a plan, I had no idea what I was doing, but I needed to take control. I decided to figure it out when I saw her.

I left the house when I knew she'd be running, my heels hitting the pavement hard. *Rage Against the Machine* in my earphones, I kept up an angry pace. My breathing was super loud, louder than usual. My heart rate accelerated with every step. My chest felt like it was constricting. The rage stuck in my throat. I couldn't swallow, and I felt like I couldn't breathe, but I kept going. I had no idea if I wanted to scare her, scream at her, or something else.

The more I ran, the more enraged I felt. Visions of her sitting in Luke's car kissing him kept going through my head. All those times I entered a room, and he was sitting next to her. The words he spoke to me last night. The words my mother spat at me. All of it ran through my mind, blasting in stereo. The same things, over and over, I couldn't silence them, no matter how much I tried. The harder I ran, the louder I heard their words.

"You aren't a good person." Luke.

"You are such a disappointment." Mom.

"You aren't special." Luke.

"Lose weight. Do your hair. At least try." Mom.

"You threw myself at me. That doesn't make you special." Luke.

"Larkin has always been better than you." Mom.

"At least Larkin is nice; you're a bitch." Luke.

"You're an embarrassment." Mom.

My shins were stinging, my thighs burning, and my cheeks were wet—from sweat, or tears, I didn't know. What did it matter? The pain I felt helped to center my anger; it gave it a voice. I started to enjoy the burning. I craved more of it. It gave me clarity. I ran faster with my chest heaving and heart exploding. All I wanted was more. I needed more of the pain and if I ran faster, I could have it. So, I did, it made me feel alive.

I saw Larkin and Brooke ahead of me. They weren't running fast at all. Brooke was probably tired from practice. *Weak!* When I saw them, I thought about how Coach Toan had hired them to be student coaches for his club team. *Of course he did; they were always his little darlings.* I could feel my rage build even more. I doubled my pace. *Fuck his darlings!*

After a block, I was finally catching up to them, but they didn't notice me. They were too busy talking and laughing. I took longer strides and approached from behind.

"Larkin!" I still had no idea what I was going to do. She and Brooke stopped and turned. I said nothing more. I felt a force rise up from deep within, I moved my arms without really thinking about it at all. I lunged, slammed my arms into Larkin's chest, and pushed her over. She fell immediately, her head bouncing off the sidewalk.

Brooke looked at me, mouth gaping, then turned her head and fell to the ground to lift Larkin's head. I stared down at the two of them. When I realized what had happened, what I had done, fear seized and jolted me. Larkin was splayed on the ground, holding her head, crying. She looked broken.

"What the HELL is wrong with you!" Brooke screamed at me red faced, rage seeping through her bulging veins.

Larkin moaned.

Suddenly, it was like I woke up and everything I had done before that moment was a fog. I hadn't been making my own decisions but had acted out of impulse somehow.

"I'm . . . I'm . . ." I backed up a few steps, then began to run.

Home. I needed to get home.

I was sure I had just screwed up my future. I messed up everything. It was over for me. Why did I do that? I had always been a bitch, sure, but I had never acted out violently. Back then, nothing I did was ever right, so it shouldn't have come as a surprise when I fucked up so majorly. I kept running. Then something came over me. The closer I got to my house, the prouder I started to feel. I thought of my mother and how she had always told me that I needed to do whatever it took to keep my status, and that's exactly what I had done. I thought she would be proud of me. I thought she'd be so proud that she might pay me a compliment. She never really did that, but maybe now I had a chance.

I picked up my pace, not because of anger, but because of pride. I was finally taking care of myself. I was standing up for myself. I thought everything would turn out perfectly. After all, it wasn't like I had punched Larkin, I had only pushed her . . . a little. What kind of person falls from a little push like that? A weakling, that's who!

. 42 .

Larkin

"What the hell just happened?" I asked Brooke.

"You don't remember?" Brooke asked, a worried look on her face.

I held my head. "Of course, I remember. But what the hell?" I said.

"I have no idea. But don't worry about her right now." Brooke sat in front of me and looked into my eyes. I knew exactly what she was doing. She was checking my pupils for signs of concussion. Then she put one finger in front of my face, "How many fingers am I holding up?"

"One."

She put up two and moved them across my face.

"Two." I rolled my eyes a bit, which admittedly hurt. "Stop. You realize concussions develop over time. Try in an hour or so."

"I know. When I had mine, it didn't get bad until a few hours later."

"I remember. That was a month before I went down. It only took you a few days to feel better after it hit you. It took me two years." I was getting frustrated. I still think it's unfair how some concussions only take a few days to heal but mine took two years. Concussions are nothing strange for female soccer players. It wasn't odd for her to have had one. The odd part was that mine had never really healed.

"I'm sorry. That was insensitive."

"No, it's okay."

"I'm just worried. Do you have a headache?"

"Yeah. Can you just help me get home?" We were a few blocks from my house, but I was afraid to walk the whole way. Honestly? I was scared I had gotten a secondary concussion and then that would be it for me. Secondary concussions can get serious. They are concussions you get on top of an existing concussion that hasn't healed. I wasn't completely healed.

"Can you call Marco?"

"Not your mom?"

"No, I don't want to worry her if I'm okay. She may lose her mind." My mother would have wrapped me in bubble wrap if she could.

"Of course. What's his number?

She dialed and talked to him. I could only hear her side of the conversation.

"Marco, it's Brooke. Larkin's friend?"

"Yeah, we need your help. She, um, fell."

"Well, yeah. We were out running when Reagan came out of nowhere and pushed her. It wouldn't be such a bad thing, but Larkin fell and hit her head."

"Yeah."

"We're on Courtland."

"No, she didn't lose consciousness or anything."

"No, I don't think she needs to go to the ER. Can you just come get us?"

"Okay. Thanks."

"He'll be here soon," she said and sighed. "Here, drink some water." She grabbed the water bottle I had dropped when Reagan knocked me over.

I took a few sips. "Thank you," I said. "Thank you for being here right now. What would I do if you weren't?"

"Well, you would have called me. Don't be silly."

"I know, but it could it have been worse. Would she have done more to hurt me?"

"I really don't know. But let's not worry about that right now. Okay?" She gave me a reassuring look, "I'll deal with her."

Marco pulled up quickly. He got out of his car without even shutting it off or closing the door.

"Larkin!" he said as he ran and kneeled in front of me. "Look at me. How many fingers am I holding up?"

"I'm fine, Brooke already did the concussion check. I'm just a little woozy." I rubbed my head. "I just need to go home and get some sleep."

"You can't sleep with a concussion. You could go into a coma," he pleaded.

"That's not true. That's like an old wives' tale. Research shows that sleep is the best thing," Brooke said, rolling her eyes. "It's amazing how much misinformation is still out there."

"Are you sure?"

"Yes, I'm sure. Girls who play soccer know how to deal with a concussion," Brooke said, standing. "Help me get her up and into your car."

"I can get up on my own. It's not that bad," I said back.

"Okay, try it, tough girl," Brooke said, not believing me at all.

"No, don't try it, let me help," Marco begged.

"Marco stop, she says she's got this."

I tried to stand up, but the dizziness took over. I sat back down before everything went black.

"Right, let us help you now," Brooke said after she leaned down to look me in the face.

"Fine!"

"Marco, help me get her in the car." Brook put her arm under my arm.

"No, I can do better than that." Marco bent down, wrapped one arm under my legs and used the other to support my back. He picked me up and quickly got me in the car. After I was settled, he turned around to Brooke, "You coming?"

"Um, yeah! Cool," she looked shocked.

The only thing I remember after that was leaning my head back on the seat and closing my eyes.

. 43 .

Reagan

When I burst through the door, I was actually starting to feel good about myself again. This was what my mom always wanted, for me to take control. In my mind, that was exactly what I had done.

"Mom!" I called.

"Mom!" There was no answer. I tried again.

"Mom!" Nothing.

I ran up the steps to her room. She was on the phone and shot me a look that could kill. "Reagan, obviously I'm on the phone," she said with scorn in her voice, then shushed me away with her arms.

I went to my room and waited for her. It took a while, but that was to be expected with my mom. I had to be patient for her to find the time to talk to me.

Ten minutes later, she finally stomped into my room.

"Reagan, you CAN NOT just barge into my room like that. I take a lot of important phone calls."

"Sorry."

"You better be. How do you think I provide for all of your spoiled needs?"

"Sorry, Mom. I'm sorry."

"What did you want?"

I shouldn't have said a thing. The look in her eyes meant she was angry. I was usually good at keeping my mouth shut when she had that look in her eyes, but not that day.

"Mom, I took care of the problem."

"What problem is that?" she asked with a sigh.

"I followed Larkin and I handled it."

"Reagan," she said, sighing again, "what did you do?"

"I ran up behind her, called her name, and pushed her."

My mom's eyes popped out of her head.

I could tell she wasn't happy, so I tried to make it better before she completely flipped out on me. "Not hard, just enough to scare her."

"Not hard? She's a head injury patient!" she started pacing. "What the HELL were you thinking?" Still pacing. "A soft wind could blow that girl over! And you just decided to push her?" she screamed. "Now I'm going to have to call her MOTHER? A woman I have despised for YEARS? And APOLOGIZE for something my stupid daughter did? How dare you put me in this position." She stopped pacing long enough to take a deep breath before she asked, "Did she fall?"

"What?"

"When you pushed her, DID . . . SHE . . . FALL?"

"Yes," I said meekly.

"DID SHE HIT HER HEAD?"

"I . . . I don't know."

"I can't believe this. You become more and more like your father every single day."

"Mom, please, stop."

"You've gone beyond worthless and jumped full throttle into a complete liability." She pointed her finger right in my face, "I CAN NOT wait until you go away to college, if you can still get in after this." She spit as she talked, "I have to get away from you."

She left the room and slammed my door shut. I melted to the floor, sobbing. She had always told me to do whatever I had to do to get what I needed. She said to stop at nothing. I did what I thought she wanted, but I had still failed her. I would never be good enough for her. Never. With that realization, the full weight of what I had done hit me. I felt incredibly worthless, like I wasn't worthy of life anymore. I had ruined everything. I let the whole world down. Nothing I did was ever right. Everything was wrong. All I ever wanted was for my mother to be proud of me.

I looked at myself in my full-length mirror and inspected my face. Standing there, I realized that if Luke had ever really loved me, Larkin coming back wouldn't have hurt our relationship at all. I swear, the more I stared at myself, the more and more I began looking like a monster. That's when I realized that I was actually becoming a monster. I stood for a few minutes watching this transformation, then spat at my image in the mirror.

. 44.

Larkin

I don't remember much about that night. I remember Marco carrying me up the steps to my room with Brooke giving him instructions the entire way. I remember Brooke making me drink water, and I remember Marco covering me with blankets before they left. They must have told my mother, because she came in to check on me every once in a while.

I woke up in the morning to my mother watching me from the rocking chair in my room. She must have been there all night. She rushed over to me as soon as I opened my eyes, but her voice was soft. "Larkin, honey. How are you feeling?"

"I don't know yet," I answered.

"Okay, I'm going to go make you a plate of eggs. You need protein right now."

"Mom, I'm fine. I don't feel like eating," I said slowly. I hadn't stopped to think that I hadn't eaten anything in about a day and the little I had eaten I had thrown up.

"No, you have to eat something for your brain."

"Fine."

As she left the room, I rolled over to face the wall. I didn't have a bad headache, just a dull one, but I felt like the room was spinning. I tried closing my eyes, but that only made the feeling worse. I couldn't go through this again.

My mom came back to my room with a plate of eggs and orange juice. She made me promise to eat.

"Larkin, at least take a few bites," she pleaded. "Then we'll decide if you need to take the day off from school."

"Mom. I'm fine. I can go."

"Just eat."

"MOOOOOM . . . where's my backpack?" my youngest brother yelled from the hallway.

"Okay, eat. I'll be back," she said to me.

She got up and left, closing the door softly behind her.

I looked at the eggs for a while, but I just couldn't bring myself to eat them. In the back of my mind, I knew the protein would be good for my brain, but the thought of having another concussion made me feel powerless. Not eating handed that power back to me. I dumped the eggs into a plastic bag I had in my room. I'd wait until I was alone in the house to get rid of it permanently.

Once I was positive everyone else was downstairs, I grabbed the glass of orange juice and bag of eggs and took them to the bathroom to dump in the toilet. When I flushed, I thought about the two times I made myself throw up. Part of me wondered if I was taking it too far, but I just didn't care. I wanted control, not food. The food felt horrible in my mouth. I wanted my body back. I wanted my life back. I saw something in the mirror I didn't like, evidence that my body had betrayed me. I wouldn't eat. I couldn't. I didn't want to. Everyone told me it was because of the head injury, but in reality? I was just stubborn. I wanted to do things my way.

I heard a knock at the bathroom door. "Larkin, are you okay?"

"Yes, Mom. I'm fine. My empty plate is on my bed."

"Okay. Good," she said.

I heard her sit outside the bathroom door. She suspected something wasn't right, I knew that. When I came out, she looked relieved.

"Okay, how are you feeling? Do you think you should stay home today?"

"No, I'm fine." Admittedly, I was woozy, but my headache wasn't too bad, and I had no problems seeing. I wasn't planning to tell her about the dizziness.

"I'll be calling the school to let them know and to inform them of what Reagan did."

"Mom, please just let it be. I'll be fine."

If there's one thing I knew for sure, girls like Reagan would lash out if they got in trouble because of you.

"I'll also be calling her mother."

"Mom, seriously?" I pleaded with her. "Please just let it be. I'm fine. If you call, I'll just look weaker than I already am. I'm almost 18; let me deal with this."

"How in the world are you going to deal with a girl that acts out violently? You can't."

"Mom, just . . . please?"

"Sorry, Larkin. I'm a mother and I have to take care of my child. It's my job."

"Fine."

She turned and walked a few steps, then turned back around.

"If you start to feel even remotely bad, please have the school call me? I'll come get you."

"Okay."

"Love you, Lark."

She left the house with my brothers following behind.

My phone rang. The high-pitched ringing pierced my brain. I grabbed my head and silenced the phone. Then, I looked at it to see who called. That's when a text came in.

***

Marco: I just tried calling. How are you feeling?

Larkin: I'm okay, not great, but I've been much worse.

Marco: Are you going to school?

Larkin: Yes, but I might not stay the whole day.

Marco: Okay, I'm coming to pick you up. Did you eat?

Larkin: Yes. I'll see you in a few.

***

I went back in the bathroom to get a quick shower. The streams of water hitting where my head hit the sidewalk hurt like crazy. I reached back to feel how bad it was. The lump was huge. She could have really hurt me. Why would she have done that? Then I remembered that Reagan had texted me a warning.

***

Reagan: Watch your back!

***

She had planned her attack. Why? She knew I wasn't interested in Luke anymore. She knew I would never play soccer again. *What was her problem with me?*

. 45 .

Reagan

Izzy honked her horn to let me know she was waiting for me. Quickly throwing on my sneakers, I ran out to meet her. The air was thick with a fog that made it hard to see more than a few feet in front of my face. Everything felt incredibly heavy, the air, the heat, my emotional state.

I opened the door to her red car and got a welcome blast of cold air. Her radio was playing loudly, as always.

"Hey, girl!" Izzy said with a smile on her face. "You okay this morning?"

"I guess?" I flashed her a sheepish look. "I think I did something stupid," I said as I sat down in the passenger side seat.

"You? No way," she shook her head no.

"Yeah. I did," I said.

"Okay. Spill."

"I was so angry after seeing Luke. I wasn't thinking clearly."

"You egged his house?" she asked. "Because I'll be pissed if you did that without me."

"Oh God, I wish that was it," I sighed, "The only thing I can describe it as is 'roid rage, and I'm not even on 'roids."

"This sounds worse than I thought. Go on."

"I followed Larkin and Brooke on their run," I said, then reluctantly finished. Izzy turned down her stereo. I think that was when she realized how important this was. "And I ran up behind Larkin and pushed her over."

Izzy laughed, "Wait, that's it? I thought you were going to say you punched her."

"I mean, I probably would have if Brooke wasn't there." I looked out the window. It was obvious Izzy did not think this was serious. "Iz, when she fell, she hit her head. I mean, I don't think she hit it hard, but she did hit it."

"Reagan, if that's all you did to her, she's lucky."

"I feel guilty. I wasn't even angry at her. I was angry at Luke."

"Yeah. Who knew he was such a dick? But I mean you saw them KISS, so . . ." she nodded. "Look, don't worry about it. You've seen some of the girls fight at school; they get serious. Hair being pulled, scratching, punching. You pushing her is no big deal." She put her car into reverse. "I mean, yeah, you lost your temper. We all do. If you feel really bad about it just apologize." Izzy said, then started laughing again. "If she doesn't run away from you, that is. I mean, I may even be a little afraid of you now!"

"Izzy. This is serious. I've always been a bitch, but it's been back hand-ed things, like starting rumors, being rude, or making fun of people."

"Right, and kind of passive aggressive," she inserted.

"Yeah, thanks for that," I said, rolling my eyes at her. "I've never acted out in violence. I didn't have control of myself." I looked at her. "I mean, I REALLY didn't have control."

"Okay, look. I get it. I do. You're feeling some degree of guilt, cut yourself some slack. You were upset and in this 'roid rage thing," she said with a wave of her hand, "whatever that means."

"Iz, I pushed a sick person, all because of a guy that was never worth it. In fact, I'm pretty sure he cheated on me the entire time. Have you seen him with those freshman girls? They throw themselves at him."

"You're probably right, but the damage is done," she nodded. "I just want to point out again that you saw them kissing in the school parking lot."

"I know, but she really is into this Marco guy. Do you see the way they look at each other? I have a feeling the kiss was more Luke than it was her," I said, then sighed. "I need to do something. Iz, I really don't think she did anything wrong."

"Reagan, I have no idea what's going on right now. You growing a conscience is too weird! Seriously, just wipe your hands and move on. When it all comes down to it, it was just a push. Seriously." I could tell she was rolling her eyes again as she said that. "You're being super dramatic right now."

We ended up driving into the school parking lot behind Marco and Larkin. Their car was going obnoxiously slow. I was sure it was because they noticed it was me in the rear-view mirror. I felt like I was going to be sick.

"Ignore them."

"I can't. I have to say something."

"Don't. I'm telling you, ignore them. Marco's being a dick right now. He knows it's us."

We pulled into Izzy's regular spot. I saw Luke out of the corner of my eye standing in front of a freshman leaning up against his Jeep, kissing her.

"Do you see them?" I asked

"Yeah. Jackass. So, ignore them, too. Ignore everyone today."

"He wasted no time."

"She's that freshman who always follows him around, she was just waiting for you guys to break-up. Seriously, not worth it. You'll be in college next year, dating college guys, and he'll still be dating a high school freshman." She waved her hand as if she smelled something bad, "It's sad."

"Today is going to suck," I said accentuating the S.

. 46 .

Larkin

Marco drove to school slower than normal that day. He was being careful not to hit any potholes, turning corners slowly, and going at least five miles below the speed limit, sometimes more.

"Marco, it's okay. I'm not THAT dizzy. You can drive normally," I pleaded.

"Nope, I'm too freaked out. If I get into an accident or have to stop fast with you in the car? Just no."

To be honest, I was feeling really lightheaded, but I didn't want him to know how bad it was.

"Okay, fine." At least we were going a little faster than the busses.

"It's not like we are late, don't worry," he tried to assure me.

It annoyed me, but I knew he was just trying to be careful.

I looked at him and said, "Thank you for caring," in the exact same way I would have said it to my mother. I was tired of being a patient. I wanted to be more than that.

"Of course, I care. Honestly, I'm surprised you're even going to school," he said. "Seriously, with your history, you should have just stayed home. I predict one hell of a headache later." He pulled the car onto the road leading to the school, "When that happens, come and get me. I'll drive you home."

"It wasn't that big of a deal, Marco." I hated the lectures. I hated when everyone saw me as weak, absolutely hated it.

"Well, considering the fact you couldn't walk on your own when I came to get you? Yeah, it was."

If I hadn't been feeling like such crap, I would have gotten mad at that. But my headache was piercing and making me feel nauseated, and the sun was hurting my eyes even though it was cloudy and foggy. I didn't want to get upset, so I turned my face towards Marco, leaned my head back.. We drove in silence the rest of the way.

I noticed Marco looking into his rear-view mirror a lot. He also slowed down his pace. I wondered what he was looking at, so I turned my head slightly to see what the problem was. It was Reagan and Izzy, but I felt so dizzy that I didn't care. I didn't mention it; Marco didn't either.

When we got to his spot, he pulled in slowly, of course. Then turned to me, "Let's wait a little bit before we go in. Okay?"

"Why?

"I just want to make sure you are okay."

"Okay," I said softly, then closed my eyes again. I didn't realize at the time that he was trying to keep me away from Reagan. I didn't care, I just wanted to keep my eyes shut for as long as I could.

After the first late bell rang, he touched my hand gently. "Are you sure you're okay to go in?" he asked, looking at me intently. "I can drive you back home."

"Marco, I'm fine. I can do this. This is nothing in comparison."

He turned off his car, got out, then ran around to open the door for me. When the door opened, I could feel the heat and humidity waft into the car. When I stepped out, I could feel the heat rising off the black parking lot.

We walked into school hand in hand. The air weighed me down. It was hard to move. I didn't tell Marco how I was feeling, he would have made a big deal out of it. Plus, he would have just gotten Brooke involved and then Brooke would have called my mother. I didn't want to be that person anymore. I wanted to be strong. So, I tried to ignore my body and just focus on his hand in mine.

Once we got into the school building, the coolness of the air was welcome, but the constant talking, lockers slamming, and doors were so loud it felt like my head was going to break open. The lights seared through my eyes. I needed to hide somewhere.

"Marco, I'm going to hit the girl's room. I'll catch up with you later," I said, then squeezed his hand to let him know I was okay.

"Are you okay? Do you want to go to the nurse instead?"

"Marco, I have to pee, that's all," I lied.

He squeezed my hand and gave me a light kiss on the cheek. "Okay Phil. I'll see you in a few."

I could not get out of that hallway quickly enough, but my legs just wouldn't take me there easily. I didn't have the energy. It felt like I was walking through heavy, wet cement. Once I finally reached the door to the girl's restroom, it took all the energy I had to open it. I thought if I could just sit down for a little, maybe with my head between my legs, I would feel better. This didn't feel like a concussion. It felt entirely different. It felt like my body was simply too heavy for my soul to keep it going.

The bathroom was quiet, but it had the overwhelming stench of bleach. My nostrils burned. The flickering fluorescent light cut through me. I opened the door to the first stall I came to. As I went in, everything started going black. I heard someone scream my name.

"Larkin!"

. 47 .

Reagan

I decided to go the long way to my locker to avoid Larkin. The fact that taking that path would also help me avoid Luke and his new girlfriend was an added bonus. I wasn't ready to apologize to Larkin yet. I knew I needed to, but I had to gather my thoughts a little more before facing her. As for Luke, I just didn't want to see him kissing all over some fourteen-year-old. I knew it was over and I didn't want him back, but I still didn't want to see him kissing little girls. How he treated me at the pool party and at his house, just like so many other times, made me realize exactly what he was: a fake. He had been a fake the entire time he was with me. He wasn't worth it anymore. He certainly wasn't worth what I did to Larkin. I was better off with no one than with him.

When I rounded the corner, I heard screams coming from the girl's bathroom.

Everyone stopped talking and stared at the door. I ran into the bathroom to find out what was happening. I swung the door open, but I was not ready for what I saw. Brooke was on the floor crying, cradling Larkin in her arms. She heard the door when I opened it and turned to see who came in.

"YOU! YOU DID THIS TO HER!" Brooke yelled at me. "GET AWAY FROM US!"

The look of hatred on her face was beyond anything I had ever seen.

"I didn't. I- I'm sorry." I turned and ran out of the bathroom. I ran in between the masses of students standing outside of the restroom door, waiting to hear what was happening. They tried to stop me to ask questions, but I pushed them out of my way. I needed to fix what I had done. For the first time in my life, I needed to help someone else.

After making my way through the crowd, I ran down the steps and barged into the nurse's office yelling, "Please, come. Larkin Phillips is unconscious in the bathroom."

The nurse stood up and followed behind me to the bathroom, weaving in and out of students. "Call 911!"

I dialed.

"What's your emergency?" the operator asked.

"She's unconscious."

"Who is?"

"Larkin Phillips. I'm at the high school, in the bathroom in the B-wing on the second floor, near the back entrance."

Brooke looked up at me, her face was red, and her eyes were teary. But they were also sharp and full of hatred, for me. When she noticed I had brought help, her face softened and her focus shifted. Larkin was still passed out in her arms. She looked like a doll. Lifeless. For the first time I really looked at her. Not at who I thought she was, but at who she was that very moment. I'd seen her in a bikini, but I had hated her and that changed what I saw. Now, she looked tiny, helpless . . . sick. I held my breath.

"What happened?" the nurse asked, kneeling down beside the two of them, grabbing Larkin's wrist to check her pulse.

"I'm not sure, I was walking in when I saw her fall. She hit her head on the floor, hard." Brooke choked back a sob and struggled to talk through her tears.

The nurse leaned down to check Larkin's breathing. She touched Larkin's face; Larkin let out a small sound. Brooke started crying even harder. Larkin was coming back. I felt like I could breathe again. I hated her, but I never wanted this.

"Larkin? Larkin, can you hear me?" the nurse began asking. Larkin nodded her head slightly.

"Okay, don't move. Reagan called an ambulance. It's on the way."

"Reagan?" Larkin said in a small voice.

"Yes, she helped," Brooke told Larkin, but shot me a quick, dirty look.

"Okay, Reagan, you did the right thing. Thank you. You should either go to class or go sit in the guidance office. The ambulance will be here soon, and they'll need the bathroom cleared out."

"O-okay," I said, then moved toward the door to make my way out of the bathroom. I turned just before I opened the door. "I'm sorry," I said barely above a whisper. No one reacted. My apologies meant nothing.

I opened the door, then walked through the hallway with tears streaming down my face. People were still gathered around, watching the bathroom door, looking to me for answers. I gave them none.

"Reagan, what's going on?" someone asked. I didn't even acknowledge them.

I walked the hallway slowly, in a daze.

I did this to her. This is my fault. This was me.

I prayed and prayed she would be okay. The girl I had wanted to hurt the day before, was lying in the middle of the girl's room, and it was my fault. I was not prepared for that kind of guilt. I hadn't wanted her to actually get hurt. I was just so upset and spun up that I hadn't been thinking.

I walked out of the building and sat on the sidewalk. No one was out here; they weren't allowed to be. I was safe from prying eyes, gossip, and questions.

Who would go out of their way to hurt someone that was already injured and hurting? Who would do that? A monster, that was who. That monster was me.

I heard the door swing open.

"Reagan, what's going on?" It was Izzy. I wasn't ready to talk.

I quickly wiped away my tears. "Nothing," I replied. "Can I just be alone right now?"

"I just, I heard the scream, then I saw you running to get the nurse."

"Please, just leave me alone," I begged.

Izzy didn't listen, she came and sat next to me.

"Do you want to bag school and go somewhere? It's kind of hot out here and my car has air conditioning."

"I can't move right now," I answered.

"Can I ask you something?" Izzy asked me.

"No."

"Is it Larkin in the bathroom? Is something wrong with her?"

"Yes."

"You're blaming yourself, aren't you?"

"Could you just go?" I snapped.

"Look, there is something else going on with her, there has to be. She's been looking more and more pale each day." She put her arm around my shoulders. "I really, in my heart of hearts, do not believe this is your fault."

I started to weep. "So, what you are saying is that sure, it might not be my fault, but that yes, I pushed a truly sick person."

"Stop. We all make mistakes. Just stop this," she said sternly. "You are one of my best friends and . . ." She stopped mid-sentence when we heard the siren of the ambulance.

"Luke is right, I'm a horrible person."

"Look, you have your whole life for self-pity, but right now is not the time," she said standing up. "Right now you have to lead the paramedics to Larkin. Do you think you can do that?"

I nodded.

"And now you are helping her. See? You're changing already." She put her hand in front of me to help me up. "Wipe your damn tears; you have a job to do."

The ambulance pulled to a complete stop right in front of us.

. 48 .

Larkin

I laid quietly on the ER bed, listening to the machines beeping around me. I was so incredibly cold. My mom thought I was sleeping and kept getting up to touch my head, cheeks, and hands. I just kept my eyes closed. I didn't know what happened to me, and honestly, I didn't care, I just felt awful and I wanted it to stop. I had an IV in my arm, pumping a clear liquid into my veins. I felt so cold.

I kept my eyes closed when the doctor came into my room.

"Is she still sleeping?" he asked my mom while touching my foot.

"I think so. She moves every once in a while," my mother said in a hushed tone.

"I took a moment to look over her records. She had a head injury two years ago, treated here?"

"Yes."

"How has her progress been?"

"Good enough for her to go back to school this year," my mom answered.

"Has she hinted at feeling worse lately?"

"No, but she has been throwing up."

"I see in her records that she's been seen for an eating disorder?"

"Yes."

"The reason I ask is because as I stand here looking at her, she's very skinny." He touched my foot again. "I'm going to order some blood tests."

"She is having problems eating. It's something we are all battling as a family . . . together."

"Has she been eating?"

"She cleans her plate."

"Sometimes anorexics become very good at hiding food."

"Yes, but . . ."

He cut my mom off. "You said she's been throwing up lately. Any chance she's making herself throw up?" His voice was caring, but with an edge.

My mom started to cry, "I think so. When she throws up, I sit outside the door. She never seems sick when it happens." She sniffled "I should have barged in the bathroom. I missed the signs."

"Okay, I'm going to have a psychologist come down and talk to the two of you. As soon as she's awake, I want to get her weighed and I want to take a look at her throat."

"Okay."

I kept my eyes closed. I knew what was going to happen next. I'd been living on nothing.

This wasn't Reagan. This was 100% me. I knew I would be admitted. They always threatened that. I kept my eyes closed a little longer listening to my mother cry, a sound I would never forget. Then I heard her pick up her phone:

"Can you come?"

I knew she was talking to my dad. I couldn't hear him.

"Okay. I'll let them know you are on your way."

"No."

"I know."

"Yes."

"I think she's been making herself throw up."

"No, she's still asleep."

"I think they'll admit her this time."

"Okay. Just get here quickly."

I could hear her put her phone down while I slowly opened my eyes. "Mom?" I whispered.

She quickly rose and hugged me. "How are you feeling?"

"I have a headache."

"Just keep your eyes closed. The doctor is sending some specialists to see you, okay?" she said using her sympathetic voice.

"Okay."

"We will get you better."

I could see the pain in her face. Her eyes were red, and her cheeks were puffy. It was obvious that she'd been crying for a long time.

The IV in my arm was making me cold, the lights were hurting my head, and I felt weak.

My father arrived quickly.

My mother looked at him and whispered, "shhh."

"We need to get to the bottom of this now," he demanded.

"She just needs rest," my mother pleaded.

"She needs to eat!" he snapped. I hated when my dad was that angry. When he gets really scared his emotions show as anger.

"Stop. The past two years have been traumatic for her. I'm not surprised she's exhibiting something like this."

"No, she needs to eat and that's final!" he yelled.

"Daddy?" I sat up.

He was mad until I called out to him. Then he melted.

"Larkin, honey," he said as he came and sat on the bed next to me.

"Why won't you eat? Please? We've been through the head injury, which wasn't your fault and couldn't be helped. But eating? You can eat. You can control this." His eyes pleaded with me.

"I don't know. I don't know why I'm doing this."

That was when two kind looking doctors came in the room.

"Larkin, how are you feeling?" one of them asked, sitting down on the edge of my bed.

"Tired," I replied.

"I'm Dr. Shah and this is Dr. Sim. We just want to talk to you for a little bit, is that okay?" she asked me.

"Okay."

"Hi, Larkin," the short, stalky doctor said. "Can you talk to me about what happened at school this morning?"

"I was kind of feeling dizzy all morning. I went into the restroom at school and just blacked out." As I talked, Dr. Sim took notes on her computer.

"We looked in your records and noted that you had a head injury two years ago. Can you tell us what happened?" Dr. Shah asked.

"I was the soccer goalie at a tournament. I got kicked in the head." So many doctors asked the same questions. Over and over again I've said the same things. To this day, I don't like talking about it. I wish they would stop asking. I just wanted to move on with my life. I still do.

"Were you knocked unconscious?"

"Yes."

"What can you tell us about the extent of your injuries?"

"I had a fractured skull and a severe concussion that turned into Post-Concussion Syndrome."

"Can you tell us about how you healed?"

"It took two years. At first, I couldn't walk without falling over; light and sound bothered me, I couldn't write; and I forgot some things that happened in my past."

"Do you remember getting kicked?"

"No."

"You went to physical therapy?"

"Yes, to work on my balance so I could walk." I hated physical therapy; it always made my headache worse. "My mom worked with me on remembering how to write, my math facts, stuff like that, the things that would come back to me later. Then they hired a tutor. But I spent most of my time in my room, in the dark."

"How long were you in your room, in the dark?"

"For the whole two years, except for doctors' appointments. There were a lot of those."

"What did you do those two years, besides appointments and sleeping."

"I read a lot. Books were my friends."

"Was reading approved by your doctor?" Dr. Shah wrote something in her file.

"No. But I couldn't look at screens, without getting a searing headache, not even my phone or my computer or my TV. I had to do something."

"Mom and dad, can we have a moment with your daughter?"

"No, we need to know what's happening," my dad snapped.

"We need to have her talk openly with us, and sometimes teens don't want to do that in front of their parents."

"Come on, let's go," my mom said, placing a calming hand on my father's arm. "You'll come and get us when you are finished?" she asked with a nod.

"Yes, and then we'll talk to all of you as a family."

My father looked like he was going to explode as my mom guided him out of the room.

"Larkin, I'm going to ask you some very hard questions. I need you to answer honestly. "While you were in bed for those two years, how did you feel emotionally?"

"I didn't feel. I was dealing with the headache."

"Did you feel in control of your life at all?"

"I mean, no. How could I be in control? Every time I tried to do something I would end up in more pain. My body felt like a jail cell."

"Is that why you stopped eating? For control?'

"It started out that way, yes, but it's more than that. I was an athlete before. I was in shape. The more I laid in bed, the more I realized how out of shape I was becoming. Then I realized I would never play soccer again. My life was finished. Everything I worked so hard for was gone." I felt like I was going to cry. I was already in therapy; I knew the reasons.

"Larkin, I have a few more questions to ask you, and you need to answer them honestly. Can you do that for me?"

"Yes." Then they asked me a string of question about how I felt about life, about my anxiety, and about how I deal with stress. They asked me about my temper and my friends. They asked about my emotional state since going back to school and even about my relationship with my parents and brothers. The list went on and on.

Finally, a nurse came in the room. "Hi, Larkin, I'm Nurse Ann. The ER physician wanted me to weigh you when you woke up," she said, then looked to the doctors. "Do you mind if I weigh her quickly, we are trying to get her admitted. There's a bed available."

"Admitted? Why?" I asked.

"Sure, we'll come back." Dr. Shah passed an annoyed look at the nurse before she looked at me and said, "Larkin, you are going to be admitted. We need to make sure you eat. You will be watched closely for a few days to make sure you are getting what you need. If you don't start putting food into your body, your body will start shutting down. We've already talked to your pediatrician and your therapist. Everyone believes this is the best course of action. This is serious. Do you understand?"

I started crying. I didn't answer them.

"We'll be back, okay?"

I kept crying.

The nurse held out her hand to help me out of bed and into a wheel-chair. I was dizzy just from getting into the wheelchair. She wheeled me to the scale and helped me up once more. "I'm going to help you get on the scale, but then I'll have to let go, okay?"

"Okay."

When she let go, I felt like I was going to fall, but I managed to keep my balance. I stood on the scale and watched the numbers as they appeared. Eighty-nine pounds. *Well, at least I had met my goal.* The nurse did not say a word about what I weighed.

She measured my height and said, "Five feet, eight inches. Okay, let's get you back to your room."

She helped me off the scale and back into the wheelchair. We passed a room with an older man moaning. Then there was a child sitting up in a bed with a bandage around his arm. Then a younger woman throwing up. But I was different, I had chosen to end up there.

Once we got back to my room, the nurse helped me up and back into bed. I laid down and pulled the small sheet on top of me. The sheet was so thin, there was no way it would keep me warm. I was freezing.

My parents walked into my room smelling like coffee. My mom put her purse on the chair, "Honey, the doctors said they'd be right back, and we could be in the room with you again when they talk to us." She came over and climbed on the bed next to me, cradling me like when I was small. My dad stood on the other side of me.

"Larkin, I brought you a pastry. Would you please try it?" I was there because I wasn't eating. I knew I needed to try.

"Okay." I held out my hand as he placed the cellophane wrapped pastry in it. When I opened it, the sound of the wrapper made my head hurt. I didn't react to it though. I didn't want to worry them anymore than I already had.

"We will get through this. Okay?" my mom kissed the top of my head. "You just have to make sure you do your part."

While my mom spoke, my dad sat silently looking out the door towards the nurse's station. My dad is never silent, never sullen. I didn't want to do this to my parents.

I slowly ate a few bites. I only did it for them. The thought crossed through my mind that they could have brought me carrots or something, but I got it out of my head. They just went to a vending machine and got whatever they could. The danish was sickeningly sweet, but it was a gesture.

Dr. Shah came back to my room alone. "Hello, Mr. and Mrs. Phillips. We had a nice conversation with Larkin. I'd like to go over some things with you and your daughter."

She talked with us for a long time. They were concerned about my weight, obviously, and they wanted to keep me to make sure I would eat and get some therapy. They told my parents that they wanted to monitor me for depression and anxiety. *I mean, of course!* Being stuck in bed from fifteen to seventeen? It's going to mess with your mind.

Then Dr. Shah said the words I never expected to hear, the words that shocked me back to reality. "Larkin, I need you to understand something.

If you don't take this seriously and begin eating, we will have to give you a Nasogastric feeding tube."

She went on to explain that a Nasogastric tube is a tube that goes from your nose to your stomach, and they feed you through it to make sure your organs don't start to fail while you are getting treatment and dealing with the psychological side of things. I was stunned. I couldn't believe I was that bad. I'm not sure I WAS that bad. But she said it and it was out there. My goal became staying as far away from the feeding tube as I could get.

"Oh God," my mom said. Silent tears fell from her eyes.

"I only say that so you realize how serious this is, and so you can make the change yourself. It's going to be hard, but we are all in this for you. Do you understand?"

"Yes," I replied, terrified.

"Mr. and Mrs. Phillips, do you have any questions?" she asked, directing her attention away from me.

As my parents rattled off their long list of questions, I went into my own thoughts. I knew they were talking, but I paid no attention to what they were saying. I went from feeling completely numb and not thinking at all, to rapid fire thoughts. A slight panic began to set in. I thought back over time, trying to figure out why I had let this happen. I never meant for it to get this bad. It was all the little things that just kept adding up. First, I got in the habit of throwing food away when no one was looking. Sometimes I would put food in a baggie so I could throw it away later. But I kept pushing it to the next level. I knew it was becoming a problem, but I couldn't, I wouldn't stop. For the past few months, I used running as a punishment for eating. Then I purged and it all fell apart. I knew what I was doing to myself. I was shocked at how far I had pushed it.

I used to be strong. I used to eat a lot on purpose to build muscle. I was never fat, but I was always large. I had to be, I was a goalie. I looked down at my body lying in the ER bed, hooked up to wires and tubes; I couldn't even find myself. My arms looked like that of a skeleton's; my hands were bony. I was pale, I was always cold, and I was dizzy most of the time. I knew being in the hospital was necessary, but I didn't want to be there. I knew I needed to fix myself, I just didn't know how.

Over the next two hours, I was given a bed in the hospital. It was clear that my roommate had spent a lot of time there. White Christmas lights hung around the room along with photo frames full of pictures of what appeared to be family. There was even one of a beautiful ballerina in a pink gown and silver toe shoes that looked somewhat like her. I did a double take. The photo was of Erin, that friend who I grew up with. The one who I used to run to the bus stop with. The one who moved when we were in fourth grade. It was Erin in the picture! I knew it because I had the same photo. She had sent it to me when I was 12.

Erin! How in the world did we end up being in the hospital at the same time, for the same thing, and in the same room? She was skinnier than me. Her appearance was jarring. She was no longer the same chubby cheeked girl I loved. She was sitting on her bed with a book on her lap, her cheeks were withdrawn, her eyes sunken. Her clothes hung on her as if she were a pole. It shocked me deeply.

"Erin?" I asked quietly. She looked at me closely.

"Oh, my god! Larkin?"

I gasped and ran to her bed as she stood. We held on to each other tightly. "What happened? I thought you moved to Minnesota."

"We moved back. My dad got out of the military and is teaching in Carlisle." We broke our hug, both sobbing. "Wait, what are you doing here? Do you have an eating disorder? Is that why you're here?"

I had never admitted it before, I had never thought of myself in that way. "I . . . I guess so?" It felt strange saying it, but if I said it, maybe I could get control over it. I needed to say the word itself. "Yes, I guess I am anorexic."

"Welcome to the club," she said in an oddly proud way. "Do you want to know the tips and tricks?"

"Okay?"

"Nurse Hatchetface, that's what we call her anyway, her last name is Hatchet. She's not nice and knows all the games in the book, so Hatchet suits her. Don't try to hide anything from her. She'll be here in the morning, so you better just make sure to eat the eggs and fruit she gives you." She looked up at the ceiling thinking of more to say. "Nurse Ritchey is very nice, she's younger and is a lot of fun. Oh," she looked at me with a sly smile, "Dr. Scott is hot. You'll love him." We both laughed. "He has dark hair, bright blue eyes, the most amazing goatee, and he definitely works out."

"This is good information to have," I nodded.

"They watch you eat. Every single little bite. Everything is measured carefully, and they know. So, some girls just puke in the stairwell. They don't usually get caught."

That was not the kind of advice I expected.

"I think I'm okay. I think I want to try to eat," I said out loud as a way to convince myself. "Do you puke in the stairwell?"

"I'll never tell, but if you puke in a bathroom they will know," she said to me with wide eyes.

"I don't want that."

"Okay. Well. If you are actually going to give it a go . . . do you have a boyfriend?" she asked.

"I'm dating someone."

"What's his name? Is he cute?"

"Marco, and yeah, I think he's cute."

"All boys named Marco are cute," she said with a nod. "You have to break it off." That shocked me. "If you breakup while you are still healing and in therapy, you will backslide. I've seen it time and time again. Girls are doing great, then they are back here. It's not worth it."

"I don't think that will happen. He's a really great guy."

"They all are, but this is a lot to deal with," she said, looking me dead in the eye. "Do you mind if I listen to music sometimes? Loudly?" she asked.

I laughed, "Not at all. Are we allowed to have dance parties?" She and I always had the best dance parties.

"We have to! As long as Nurse Hatchetface isn't here."

She was still just as hilarious as I remembered. I finally felt at ease with everything. I thought that with Erin by my side, I would be okay. I could breathe again.

"I missed you so much!" I took her back into my arms for another hug.

"Me, too. You were the only one to ever really understood me. We can't lose touch again."

We had lost touch sometime during middle school. Her family moved around so much. She became more serious with ballet and I became obsessed with soccer.

"How long have you been here?" I asked her.

"I'm in and out. I haven't been successful yet. I get better, then I go home, and the stress gets to me, so I backslide again."

"Can I ask you a question?" I asked her. I needed to know about the feeding tube.

"Sure."

"They told me that if I don't get better, they will give me a feeding tube. An NG Tube?"

"Do whatever you can to not have that happen. It's force feeding."

"I don't want it. Does everyone get it?"

"No, but you know what? You are probably safe. They were probably just trying to scare you," she said. "Oh, yeah, and you get weighed every day. It's a nightmare seeing the scale numbers go up. If you really work the system, that's what will happen. If you don't want to gain, just put pennies in your pocket. One girl actually brought small rocks in her suitcase."

"They don't check for that?" I asked.

"It depends on the nurse, actually," she nodded. "They'll probably bring you something to eat soon. I'm just letting you know; they will sit with you while you eat it. It won't be a ton of food, just a small amount to start, but they will make sure you eat."

"Okay, thanks." I sighed to myself. I had to do this, but I sure did hope it was a salad. We sat and talked for another hour. I learned that she had started dieting when she was nine because her mom was always dieting. I hadn't realize that when we were little. I learned that she truly believed she was fat and that she suffered from anxiety as well.

In the photo, and my memory, Erin's cheeks were plump and pink. Her make-up covered eyes were vibrant and her slender legs were full of muscle. She told me she had a teacher who would only give the principal parts to tiny, skinny girls, so Erin made losing weight a priority. When she became too weak to continue dancing, her parents pulled her out. They hoped getting rid of the pressure to be skinny would help her in dealing with anorexia, but she only ended up in and out of the hospital. A lot of her friends couldn't deal with it and stopped calling; kind of the same way my friends didn't call me after my accident.

. 49 .

Reagan: Can we talk?

Brooke: I'm not sure what you could possibly want to talk to me about. Guilt maybe?

Reagan: I lost my temper. I'm sorry. I need to make this right.

Brooke: You think? I'm not sure what you can possibly do to make it better, though.

Reagan: I'm trying here, okay? Luke broke up with me and I became enraged.

Brooke: Obviously. You know, she doesn't even want Luke.

Reagan: I know.

Brooke: Right, so this is just insane. My best friend is in the ER, and I have no idea what's going on, and I can't get ahold of anyone to tell me how she is, and honestly? I don't give a shit about your mental state concerning your boyfriend, especially since you PROBABLY CAUSED THIS. Okay? So, please. Shut up!

Reagan: I know, I deserve that.

Reagan: The reason I'm texting is I want to talk to her and make it right.

Brooke: SHE IS IN THE HOSPITAL. I'm pretty sure she doesn't want to see you.

Reagan: I know, that's why I'm texting you.

Brooke: Like I'm going to help you?

Reagan: I need to make it right.

Brooke: Yeah, you do, but your timing is spectacularly horrible. YOU are spectacularly horrible.

***

Marco: Have you heard anything yet?

Brooke: Not yet.

***

Brooke: Marco is texting me. Gtg

Reagan: Okay. Does he hate me, too?

Brooke: I really don't care about your emotions right now.

***

Marco: Will you let me know as soon as you hear something?
Brooke: I will.
Marco: Okay, look. I'm worried about something.
Brooke: What's that?
Marco: I don't think she eats.
Marco: I don't think this is because of Reagan pushing her.
Marco: Or maybe it does have something to do with it, but not eating has something to do with it, too. I'm sure of that.
Marco: And, honestly, she really doesn't eat, and she runs a lot. You know how much she runs.
Brooke: I know. But I took her to McDonald's, and she ate with me.
Marco: I don't know. I'm worried. Please let me know when you hear something.
Brooke: I will.

***

Brooke: I'll let you know when I hear something. Okay?
Reagan: Okay. Thank you.

***

Luke: I heard Reagan pushed Larkin and she hit her head again? Is that why she passed out? Is that what is happening?
Brooke: I really don't know anything.
Luke: Did Reagan push her?
Brooke: Yes.
Luke: Did she hit her head?
Brooke: Yes
Luke: I swear to GOD!

***

Luke: What the hell is wrong with you?
Reagan: Luke, not now.
Luke: Pushing sick people? Seriously low.
Reagan: I REALLY don't have time for this right now. You are slime, you cheated on me, then act as if I'm the whore. Go to hell.

***

Brooke: Larkin, I just want to know what's going on. Are you okay? Please call me as soon as possible.

***

L's Mom:	Brooke, I'm sorry, we are just getting Larkin settled in a room. She will be here for a little while.
Brooke:	What? Why? Oh God.
L's Mom:	She hasn't been eating and it's become a real problem.
Brooke:	But she just had a Big Mac with me.
L's Mom:	I know honey. She may be purging as well. They are going to keep her for a few days to get a handle on it.
Brooke:	So, it wasn't because she hit her head again?
L's Mom:	No.
Brooke:	Can I come visit?
L's Mom:	Give her a day. I'll let you know as soon as the doctor says it's okay.
Brooke:	Can I call her?
L's Mom:	Not yet. I'll let you know. I'm sure Larkin would love to talk to you. I have to go, but I'll keep you updated. Okay?
Brooke:	Okay.
L's Mom:	She really needs strong friends right now. I'm counting on you.

***

Brooke:	Just FYI, it doesn't seem like it's completely your fault. I thought you should know. There's something else going on.
Reagan:	Oh, thank God. But what's wrong?
Brooke:	Judging by how you made fun of her weight at the party, I'm guessing you already know.
Reagan:	She's not eating?
Brooke:	You are a GENIUS.
Reagan:	Okay, look, cut the shit. I need to make this right.
Brooke:	Right. Well, we'll see.
Reagan:	I'm being serious here. I'd like the chance to apologize to her. I'll even make a public statement and post it on social media.
Brooke:	Fine. I'll let you know if I hear anything.
Reagan:	Thank you.
Reagan:	And I'm sorry for being a bitch. I'm going to change.
Brooke:	Yeah, right. We'll see.

. 50 .

Larkin

They woke us up early the next morning. I was not expecting that.

"Larkin, I have to get your vitals now, okay?" I woke up slowly, facing a kind looking woman with dark eyes and black hair. "I have to get your blood pressure." She put a cuff around my arm and waited, smiling at me the entire time. She looked at my electrolytes drip, checked its levels, and adjusted something on the pump. She typed a few things on her laptop. "You have to be at breakfast in 30 minutes, okay? Group therapy after that," she said with a quiet voice. "Your IV is on wheels, you can take it with you." Then she turned to check on Erin.

"Erin, honey? Erin? Erin?" She tried waking Erin a few more times before checking her heart rate. She pushed the call button.

"Can I help you?" a voice said over the speaker.

"It's Nurse Ritchie, Code Blue, Erin Roberts, Bradycardia, yeah, 40 beats per minute."

I sat up in the bed. Blue lights started flashing outside of our door. Nurses came running in. A doctor followed close behind.

"What's happening?" I screamed. I was terrified.

A larger nurse with brown hair pulled the curtain to separate me from them. I had no idea what was happening. None.

Finally, everyone calmed down and I heard Erin's voice. I breathed a sigh of relief.

Thank God!

Dr. Shah ran in at that point. There was some soft talking that I couldn't really make out.

Then they started speaking directly to Erin.

"Erin, you are getting to the point where we will need to use an NG tube."

"I don't want to be tubed. Don't force feed me."

"Your body needs food, you are faking the system, and you aren't following the plan. You are gaining weight on your chart, but you are shrinking. We have to do something, or we will lose you. Do you understand what I'm saying to you?"

Sobbing.

"We'll call your parents and discuss this with them."

"Please, don't do this to me."

"Erin, you are a very sick girl. We need to do whatever we can to heal you."

I couldn't believe what I was hearing. Was this my future?

"We are bringing your breakfast to you; Nurse Taylor will sit with you while you eat," Dr. Shah said. "We don't want you alone right now, okay?"

Erin smiled at me weakly. "I am not alone, Larkin's with me."

"Larkin has to eat in the cafeteria, according to her schedule," said Dr. Shah.

"I don't want to leave her," I said to Dr. Shah who didn't know of our history. "We've been through more than this together."

"We need to make sure you both are getting the treatment you need." She looked at her watch, then said, "Larkin, you should get ready for breakfast. You can catch up with Erin a little later."

"FINE." Erin and I blurted out almost simultaneously.

Nurse Ritchie came over to my bed and said, "Larkin, you heard the doctor, it's time to get ready for breakfast. Okay?"

"Okay." I got up, feeling the cold hard tiles on my unsteady feet. When I stood, I felt a little dizzy, but I held it together. I walked into the bathroom and looked at myself before I started to wash my face. The only thing I kept telling myself was that I was nowhere as sick as she was. Maybe I was right, but it didn't matter; I was making the same decision to slowly kill myself. I just didn't see it that way yet.

I walked out of the bathroom and found Erin curled up on her side, looking out of the window, her shoulders moving up and down, with sniffles coming from her nose. She was silently crying. I wanted to run up to her and hug her.

"Go to breakfast, Larkin," the nurse told me and shushed me away. "I don't know where to go," I said, my voice small and quiet.

"Turn right out of the door, it's at the end of this hall."

"Thank you."

I slowly walked to the little cafeteria on my floor, still dizzy.

I saw so many other teens there. Mostly girls, but some boys. Some with feeding tubes, but most without. I wished I had Erin with me. I didn't know anyone, and I felt so out of place. There was no way I was anywhere near as skinny as these people. Some of them were so skinny they looked like skeletons. Some were wearing large sweatpants and hoodies. Some just looked normal. I walked up to the counter.

"Name?"

"Larkin Phillips." The nurse took my arm and checked my arm band. Then she handed me a tray which included eggs, an apple, two pieces of toast, orange juice, and a glass of water. No napkin. I knew that was to make sure I couldn't spit my food out and hide it. I took my tray and sat at the first empty table. The table was glass, completely see through. There was no way I could hide food at all. I sat and slowly ate. A middle-aged woman approached me.

"You have to eat all of it. They won't let you have coffee until you eat it all," she said looking down at me. I nodded at her.

I ate it all and calculated my calories with each bite. *Two eggs 140 calories. Toast 208 calories. Apple 95 calories. Orange juice 112 calories. So that was 469 calories for breakfast alone!* The thought of it made me feel sick; I wanted to throw up. But there was nowhere for me to do that. I needed to call my mom, but I couldn't until after dinner (*two more meals!*). I needed to go home. I felt like I couldn't be there anymore. They were nothing like me. I didn't understand.

After eating, they kept us there for a little while longer. I started to hyperventilate. I needed to get out of that room. I'd already eaten. What more did they need from me? I took my tray to the nurse hoping she would let me go.

"I ate. May I go to my room and lie down?"

"You have group therapy, an activity, personal counseling, nutritional counseling, then dinner. You can't go back to your room."

"But what about Erin? I have to check on Erin, she needs me." I cried.

"Erin is being cared for. You need to focus on healing yourself now," said the nurse.

I was a prisoner.

I spent that first day keeping quiet and being completely reserved. I didn't speak up in therapy, except for when I was forced.

I didn't belong.

I made it through the entire day, one painful experience at a time.

After dinner I called my mom crying. "Mommy, come get me, please?

"Larkin, we can't do that. You need to be there. We will come visit tomorrow."

"Mommy, I'm not like them. I'm not that bad."

"I know honey. We just need you to eat. I know you are tired of fighting it, but you have to. We need you at 100% again."

"Mom, I'll never be 100% again, I'll always have the headaches and I'll always have anxiety. Just come get me. I can't do this."

"Larkin, we love you, but we can't do that."

"Mommy, please," I sobbed. I could hear my mom crying on the other side of the call.

"Larkin, we can't. I want you home so badly, but I need you healthy and that's our priority," she said. "Honey, everyone has been calling asking about you. They are all worried, even Reagan."

"Reagan? Seriously?"

"Yes, she's called a number of times. She wants to come and see you with Brooke."

"What? Why? So, she can push me again? She feels like she didn't finish me off?"

"Larkin, I think you should listen to her; she feels horribly about what happened and how she's behaved. But don't worry about her right now," she said quickly. "Marco wants to come and see you too. He dropped some things off for me to bring to you."

"That's nice of him," I said, but my mind flashed on what Erin had said the night before . . . *break it off*. Guilt washed over me. Marco was a good guy. He only wanted what was best for me. "Just, please come get me. Please."

"I can't do that yet, but I will come see you tomorrow."

"Mommy, I love you."

"I love you too, baby."

I was sobbing as I walked back to my room. Erin was there, but her babysitter nurse was gone.

"Hey, how was your first day?" she asked with a smile, as if nothing had happened that morning at all.

"Where's your nurse?"

"Oh, they saw me eat, made sure it digested and let me go." She was hooked up to heart monitors.

I walked over to her and sat down in the chair next to her bed.

"That was scary this morning," I said.

"It happens. I'm not worried about it," she said with a wave of her hand as if it was nothing.

"Are they going to give you a tube?"

"They say they are, but I'll fight it."

"Why? It might help you."

"It's force feeding. It's a crime."

She had said this the night before, but after what happened that morning, I just wanted her to have the tube. I was scared for her.

We spent the rest of the night talking. We told each other secrets we had never told anyone. We re-bonded after time lost.

"Can I ask you something?"

"Of course, we are best friends, right?"

"Yeah! Definitely. You said I should break up with Marco. Why?"

"Because he will break your heart and then you'll end up here again." She looked down at her small hands. "It happened to me. That's why I'm here. I've been battling this for a long time now, but I was doing well for a few months, and I started dating Alex. It was great. We were together for a year. I wasn't gaining, but I wasn't losing. We started fighting, and it all came back. I couldn't stand the thought of eating. I started losing weight again. The pressure was on me with my parents. And he bailed; he couldn't handle it. I stopped fighting. I stopped trying. It was the worst it had ever been." I didn't know what to say, so I just grabbed her hand as she talked. A small tear dropped to her cheek. "I just . . . I can't eat. And no one in the world understands what's going on. I'm terrified of eating now. I'm also terrified to not eat."

"I think, I think we need to work on it together. Can you do that with me?" I began pleading. "I know we just found each other again, but I need you here on this Earth. I can't lose you again."

"I don't know if I can fight anymore."

"You can, I promise you can. I'm here with you."

"Okay," she said almost silently.

"Don't fight the feeding tube," I begged.

"Let's just change the subject," she said suddenly, then smiled. "Tell me about Brooke. I remember her, but you guys got much closer after I moved. When is she coming to visit?"

"Hopefully, soon. But I told you about Reagan last night, right?"

"Oooo, juicy, yeah."

"I just talked to my mom. She said Reagan wants to come visit me. She wants to apologize."

"What are you going to do if she shows up here?" she asked, rolling her eyes.

"Kick her out," I replied.

"Well, maybe just let her talk. She may surprise you."

"I don't know."

"Girls, it's way past lights out. Time for bed." Nurse Ritchie came in and turned off our lights.

We both laughed as I walked to my bed using the light from the hallway to guide me. I tossed and turned for the first part of the night. My stomach felt so full that it hurt. It was the first day I had eaten three meals and three snacks in a long time, I wanted it out of my stomach. I couldn't purge; the nurse's station was right outside of my room. The thought of going into the stairwell to throw up sounded good to me, but I fought the urge. It was too late, nothing was happening in the hallway, and there was no way I could get there without anyone noticing anyway. I just had to deal with it. I tried curling up in the fetal position to cradle my stomach. That just made my stomach pouch out, which made me feel fat. I tried lying flat, but the fullness was overwhelming. Finally, at some point in the night, I fell asleep.

I dreamt of Marco and our kiss in the creek. Water rushed around us, threatening to carry me away, but I felt safe wrapped in his arms as he held me tight. The water was rising up to our necks, rushing, harder, more pressure. He bent down to kiss me on the lips when the water rushed over our heads. I got colder and colder, until the water covered us completely. We stayed there kissing, not moving, not swimming, not floating, just drowning as we kissed.

Suddenly, he disappeared. It was only me in the creek, fighting for air. The sound of the water was so loud, it filled my ears with sounds of terror as I fought. The water rushing in and out of my ears began to sound like screaming and yelling. Soon it didn't sound like water at all. It was just humans screaming, and beeping, lots of beeping. I just kept trying to swim against the current, but it kept dragging me back down. I couldn't breathe. The beeping became louder. The screaming . . . "Clear . . . one . . . two . . . three" over and over again. I began to stir out of my dream. I woke with a deep breath and sat up immediately. My room was full of people. Doctors and nurses. They all surrounded Erin, yelling directions over and over again. I jumped out of bed and stood there, frozen in my nightclothes.

"Noooooooo!" My eyes exploded into tears, I knelt down on the ground. This time I knew exactly what was happening.

Two nurses ran to pick me up. They walked me out of the room, but the whole time my head was turned toward Erin, watching.

"What's happening?" I screamed, "What's happening?" over and over again. But I knew.

They walked me to the game room and sat me down with my back toward the window. I realized they didn't want me to see the flurry of activity. One nurse went back to Erin, the other stayed with me.

"We are doing what we can," the nurse said reassuringly.

I said nothing, just sat cradling my head as I wept. The nurse reached up and touched my shoulder for comfort, but she did not speak or interrupt my crying. This moment lasted only briefly, but it felt like an eternity.

Suddenly, everything went silent I turned to look. Nurses and doctors were leaving the room quietly, their heads down. I knew.

I screamed and I burst into sobs. Loud, heart wrenching sobs.

The nurse stood and put her body over mine to hug me. As I sobbed, she held on to me and rocked me. While holding me she made a phone call.

"I need to get Larkin Phillips into another room. Can we get her set up in 403?" She waited for an answer. "Yes. Okay. I'm taking her there now. Can someone bring me her things? Great. okay."

She got off the phone and said, "Larkin, we are going to switch your room. Come with me, okay? I'm going to have a doctor come and talk to you, but I'll stay with you as long as I can," she said. I continued sobbing.

As we walked out of the game room, I turned my head to look. People were going in and out slowly. We entered my new room, which was sterile and not set up yet. It was void of the flowers and Erin's framed photos on the window ledge. The nurse sat me on the bed and laid me back. Finding a blanket, she covered me. It did nothing for me; I was still shivering. I couldn't stop. I curled up in a ball, holding my legs to my chest with my back toward the nurse. She rubbed my back as I laid and cried.

A doctor I had never seen before came into the room. He was a tall, older man with graying hair, and a beard, and eyes that were spaced too closely together.

"Larkin, can we talk?"

I didn't answer him.

"I need you to try to sit up and concentrate on what I'm about to tell you."

I pushed myself up into the sitting position and looked at him without saying a word. "Erin, your roommate, has passed away."

The words cut me. I knew she had died, but to hear someone say it . . . it became too real. "She had been fighting anorexia for years and years. Her body couldn't handle it anymore. Her heart stopped this morning."

"Please, stop talking. I need my mom."

"She fought treatment; she didn't want to heal." He shook his head, then reached in his pocket and handed me his phone.

My hands shook as I put in my mom's phone number. "Mom, I don't want to be here. Please, come get me." I was sobbing.

"Larkin, I already told you that I can't, but I will be in to see you today."

"Erin died this morning."

"Who?"

"Erin, my roommate. Remember Erin from when I was little? She was here and she just died. I was there when it happened."

"I'm on my way." She hung up.

"Larkin, you have a chance to heal, take it," the doctor said looking at me intently.

"This isn't the time for lectures," I whispered. I just wanted a moment to be sad. For the past two years all I had done was fight for my life. I wanted to just sit and think. Just for one moment.

"But this is exactly the time. You see what can happen now."

"Do not turn this into a life lesson," I snapped. "She died so I could learn a lesson? That's heartless."

"That's not what I'm saying. I'm saying that you can heal, or you can let this ruin you."

"Please, leave my room."

"I'm sending someone in with some breakfast."

"I don't want to eat."

"Think of food as lifesaving medication. If Erin had eaten, she wouldn't have died. I'll have someone come in and talk to you again soon."

I shot him a dirty look right before he turned and walked out of the room. Moments later a tray of food was delivered to me. I pushed it off the bed in a rage. The nurse got up and started to clean up my mess.

"He's right. Look at food as your medication," she said sighing. "I'll go get you a meal replacement shake. Vanilla or Chocolate?"

"What?"

"If you aren't going to eat, you need to drink a meal replacement shake. So, vanilla or chocolate?"

"Chocolate," I said, collapsing back down on the hard bed.

A few moments later she returned with a chocolate shake and a straw.

I sat up again and slowly put the straw in my mouth. I took a tiny sip, then started crying again, but I forced myself to continue drinking one sip at a time. When I finished, the nurse took the bottle from me and left the room for a bit. I didn't lie down again. I sat up thinking about Erin. I kept replaying our conversations over and over again. I realized that during our entire conversation, she had been giving me warnings.

Don't be in a relationship.

If you are truly going to do this you have to find your strength within yourself, not in a boyfriend.

Eat everything they give you.

Don't let it spiral out of control.

I realized she was telling me what to do to not become her. To not get to her level. That was when my mom came running into my new room.

"Oh, Larkin, honey," she said nothing more, she just sat on my bed and held me. I felt safe in her arms. So safe that I drifted off to sleep.

. 51 .

Reagan

I felt nauseated as I sat by my front window waiting for Brooke to pull up. I had no idea what to say or do. I didn't know how to simply walk through the door to the hospital. I had no idea what I would say to Brooke on the ride there.

Brooke's car horn shook me from my thoughts. I grabbed my purse and ran out of the front door. As I approached her car, I could hear her stereo music blaring, which was unlike her.

I opened the door and the thud, thud, thud of the bass shook my body. I got in, trying not to think of my impending hearing loss.

"Thank you for taking me," I said.

"What? I can't hear you," she said, yelling over the music.

"I said . . ." I tried to yell over the music too. "Never mind," I muttered. I realized what she was doing; she was making sure that she didn't have to talk to me.

"We're going to stop and get pizza. I already ordered it." she yelled. I didn't answer her, there was no reason to.

She was driving fast. It was obvious she was agitated by my presence.

She came to quick stop in front of Nikolai's Pizza, throwing my body forward a bit, then whipped into the parking spot and slammed on her breaks.

She turned down the music and said, "Just stay here. I'll run in." She left me sitting in the car. None of this was normal for Brooke, at all.

A few minutes later, she came out holding a big pizza box and opened the car door on my side, "Here, hold this," she said and shoved the box onto my lap. The heat from the pizza burned my thighs, but I didn't dare move it.

She got in on her side, and I quickly spoke before she turned the music up again. "Thank you for bringing me."

"Well, I figure you need to face her."

"Right," I said with a sigh.

"Don't make me regret my decision," she said before she turned the music up again.

After ten minutes we pulled into the hospital parking garage. When she turned off the car. The silence felt . . . loud. We got both got out of the car with me carrying the pizza and walked to the elevator.

As we stepped inside, she gave me a quick look. "Do you even have any idea what you will say to her?"

I took a deep breath before answering, "No, I have no clue." Then I started talking before she could interrupt. "Brooke, I have been awful and I'm sorry. I didn't realize how awful I was until I saw her in the bathroom. I will make this better."

Brooke leaned back into the elevator wall, "Look, this wasn't exactly your fault. As much as I hate you, this wasn't completely you."

"Right."

"No, seriously. She's been doing this to herself. You didn't help the situation at all, and you WERE horrible to her. But this is bigger than the both of us. Much bigger."

"I, um . . ."

She interrupted me, "This is bigger than you and Luke, her and Luke, and you and your goalie position. Do you understand? Those trivial things don't matter."

"I . . ."

She interrupted me again, "This is not about you. Do NOT make this about you."

I didn't say anything. We entered the hospital and walked the wide corridors in silence. When we got to Larkin's room, Brooke hesitated and took a deep breath. Then she walked in ahead of me.

When I first saw Larkin, she was cradled in her mother's arms, still in her nightgown, her hair a mess, and her eyes bright red. It looked like she had just been put in that room; it was empty.

When she saw Brooke, she jumped out of bed and hugged her, nuzzling her face in Brooke's shoulder. They both started crying.

"Don't leave me. Please, never leave me."

"I won't ever. I promise. Never again, I swear."

When they parted, Larkin looked at me where I stood, still holding the pizza. She walked up to me, took the box, and put it on her bedside stand. I expected her to tell me to get out, or push me, or anything. But instead, she reached out her arms and hugged me. It took my breath away. As I stood there with my arms around her, I could feel how small she was. I could feel her ribs against my arms and her spine against my hands.

Before breaking our hug, she said something surprising that shook me to the core. "Reagan, I'm sorry."

"Larkin, I'm here to apologize to you."

"You don't have to. Anything can happen to any of us, at any time. I just want us to be okay."

"I do too," I agreed. "This needs to stop."

"I just don't have the energy to talk about it today, but what I do know is that this fighting isn't worth it."

"I'm just, I'm sorry. I know what I did was wrong, and I wish I could take it all back. Every single moment."

"Stop, please. We are starting fresh, right now. It's not worth it. We know what we both did. And, the reality is, if you hadn't pushed me, I may not be getting the help I need. I don't want to be here, but maybe I'm where I need to be."

She turned toward Brooke, "You don't know how much I need you right now."

We all sat down, Brooke and me in the chairs, and Larkin and her mother on her bed. We ate pizza and chatted. I watched Larkin take a bite every once in a while, but it wasn't much. A nurse came in occasionally to take note of what she ate.

"Did she use the bathroom after eating?" the angry looking nurse asked Larkin's mom.

"No, she hasn't even gotten up," her mom said before the nurse turned and walked away.

We sat and talked for a while longer, eating pizza, crying and laughing, and bearing our souls. Bonding. Larkin's mom stayed in the room talking and laughing as well. Larkin told us about what was happening, about her injury and what she did for those two years she was away. She explained how it felt emotionally, about her pain levels, and about how she was scared to go back to school. But mostly, we talked about Erin. I think Erin is the reason Larkin is still with us today. Erin's death hurt her deeply. It hasn't been an easy road for her, and she'll have to deal with her eating disorder for a long time. But that was the beginning. People always say God gives you angels, and Erin is hers.

. 52 .

Larkin

The Present

I look around at the girls surrounding me in the circle of chairs. Some are wearing maroon hoodies with Stone Valley University scrawled across the front. Some are wearing sorority t-shirts. Some are there still in sleeper pants, hair up in messy buns, obviously wanting to be someplace else.

"Don't be Erin, fight. You can do this. I beg you to do this," I say, wiping away a tear. "You don't have to be Reagan, putting up with abuse. If something is wrong, tell someone. Don't keep it locked away in your heart for years and years." I look around the room, at each and every person, just to make sure they understand me. "Don't be like me and wait to take this seriously. Take it seriously right now." A few of the girls are crying. "Understand, no matter how bad things get, you have choices to make. Make choices that enhance your life, not choices that tear you down."

"Thank you for sharing with us, Larkin. I think your story is both inspirational and cautionary," says Beth, the advisor of my eating disorder group.

"Thank you, just . . . ladies, please eat. I need all of you in this world. I can't make it without you," I plead. We all stand up and grab our backpacks.

A girl with an oversized sweatshirt on, and a backpack that looks like it weighs more than her approaches me and says, "Larkin, I'm so sorry about what happened with Erin. I can't imagine how painful that was."

"It was, and that's why I wanted to talk to you guys. I don't want any of you to end up like her. I love you all too much. I fight this every day just like you do. I'm not completely healed, and I don't think I ever will be." I give her a small hug. She feels so skinny in my arms, it makes me want to hug her harder, to give her all I have.

"What happened to Marco? Do you still talk?"

"One in a while. He went to Chesapeake College in Annapolis," I say with longing in my heart. "We are friends on social media, and we message each other once in a while. But it's less and less now that we are in college."

"That's sad. You should try to see him over summer break."

"You know what? I might."

"Where's Brooke?"

"She's at Penn State on a soccer scholarship. Reagan and I see her a lot."

We walk together out of Weber and I head to Seibert, to my dorm. I walk through the glass doors, take a right, and go down the same hallway I've been walking for the past six months. I open the fourth door on the right and walk in, throwing my backpack on my desk and flopping on my bed.

Reagan plops down on my bed next to me. "How'd it go? Am I going to have a bunch of girls hating me now?" she asks.

"Oh stop, no," I laugh. "I ended it on a good note. We may have some fans."

"Oooo, fans. I love having fans."

"Don't let it go to your head," I warn her.

"I have to get to practice," she says, sitting up. "Meet me for dinner?"

"Yes!"

"Will you get something more than a salad?" she pleads. "Like, maybe add a soup to it or something?"

"I will, I promise."

"Okay, thank you." Then she looks at me as if she just remembered something important. "Brooke called; she wants us to go visit her this weekend. You game?"

"I'm always game for a trip up to State College!" I smile. "Road trip!"

She gets up, walks to the door, and flings her soccer bag over her shoulder. "I love you, Lark, and I'm sorry."

"I'm sorry, and I love you, too," I call after her as she leaves the room. It's become a habit. We always tell each other that we are sorry, and that we love each other. It's important to us.

I put on my slides and grab my cleats, shoving them in my backpack. Then pull out the maroon mesh bag filled with small pink soccer balls out from under my bed. Throwing both over my shoulder, I spin around and flip the light switch, then open my door, the whole time going over plans for the evening practice. I walk out into the bright hallway and realize I forgot my wallet.

I sigh to myself, "Can't get the girls popsicles if I don't have money," and turn around to go back in my room. It's impossible for eight-year-old girls to NOT have a cold snack on a hot day! I may not be able to play soccer, but I love being the head coach to a group of little girls.

. 53 .

Marco: Hey, Phil. What are you up to?

Larkin: On my way to practice.

Marco: The little athletes. Tell them I said, hi!

Larkin: I will, and they'll go . . . Oooooooooooo, Maaaaarrrrco

Marco: The legendary.

Larkin: How's everything.

Marco: Good. So. Can we get together over break?

Larkin: I would like that.

Marco: I miss you.

Larkin: I miss you, too.

Marco: Larkin?

Larkin: Yeah?

Marco: I love you. I'm still waiting.

The End.

For further information about topics in this novel:

A Complete Guide to Post-Concussion Syndrome, Cognitive FX
www.cognitivefxusa.com/blog/post-concussion-syndrome-and-post-
concussion-symptoms-pcs

Anxiety and Depression Association of America
adaa.org

Brain Injury Association of America
www.biausa.org/

How to Recognize the Signs of Mental and Emotional Abuse
www.healthline.com/health/signs-of-mental-abuse

National Eating Disorders Association
www.nationaleatingdisorders.org

Abigail Wild dwells inside her dreams where creativity thrives. As a child, she focused on visual arts, but after twenty years as a graphic designer, all the stories she held captured in her mind clamored to be set free. She put down her tablet and picked up the pen. She went back to school, earning an MFA in creative writing, and began her new life's work: writing the stories of her heart. Today, Abigail is a novelist, writing coach, editor, competition judge, and writing teacher. She particularly enjoys working with emergent writers, often giving them the same pep talks she received years ago. She lives in central Pennsylvania with her husband, three children, and three budgies. The budgies, named Pablo, Prissy, and Lily, tend to make a racket while Abigail is trying to write, but she is not deterred!

Made in the USA
Middletown, DE
02 March 2021